Praise for Charisma

*Barbara Hall's writing is exquisite in this riveting glimpse into the world
of spirituality and mental illness, near death experience and the real life
search for authentic existence. With captivating characters, pitch perfect
dialogue, and a seemingly innate understanding of the Divine, Charisma
is an existential, theological and literary tour de force.*

- Rev. Andrea Raynor, Author of The Voice That Calls You Home

Charisma

Barbara Hall

Premier Digital Publishing - Los Angeles

Charisma

Copyright © 2013 Barbara Hall

eISBN: 978-1-62467-091-6
Print ISBN: 978-1-62467-092-3

Published by Premier Digital Publishing
www.premierdigitalpublishing.com
Follow us on Twitter @PDigitalPub
Follow us on Facebook: Premier Digital Publishing

"[Visionaries have] moved out of the darkness
that would have protected them, and into the dark forest,
into the world of fire, of original experience. Original experience
has not been interpreted for you, and so you've got to work life out
for yourself. Either you can take it or you can't."

-Joseph Campbell

"The woods of Arcady are dead,
And over is their antique joy;
Of old the world on dreaming fed;
Grey Truth is now her painted toy."

-W. B. Yeats

CHAPTER ONE

Before Dr. David Sutton has taken a seat across from me I have a good read on him. Middle child, insecure about his height, insecure about his lack of athleticism, he overcompensated in academics. His father never considered a degree in psychiatry a real medical degree. He's not a real doctor as one of his brothers—or worse, sisters—might be. He keeps a lid on all this by being organized and controlled and he never lets loose except for a glass or two of spirits when he comes home. The alcohol is to help him deal with his loveless relationship. His girlfriend (she won't marry him or he won't ask) is in a similar profession but does a little better than he does. She buys his clothes but he won't venture outside his two or three conservative looks and he takes back the motorcycle boots and the leather jackets and this becomes one of those things they like to joke about but his lack of adventure is festering now and she is going to the gym a lot, dreaming of fake boobs and looking around. Her name is a J name. She has curly hair but she straightens it. They never have sex.

I know all this on my own, looking at his body language and expressions. Only the name and the hair come to me as a kind of vision. I don't fire up the charisms all the time. In fact, I mostly try to keep them battened down. This is what I try to explain to people. If I could get them to stop, I would. I can't get them to stop. When you say that to caring professionals, you end up where I am, in Something Or Other Rehabilitation Center in Get Lost, California. I don't mind. I'm in the trauma ward. I don't have to be around addicts. They keep us separated. I like crazy people so much better. Addicts just lie and manipulate. Crazy people have color and imagination and the thing is, some of us aren't actually crazy, we're just right.

Dr. David Sutton has thinning blond hair and nice eyes. These are his calling card. His resting face is a poker face. This is something he taught himself.

"Hello, Ms. Lange. I'm Dr. David Sutton."

"I know."

He smiles and writes.

"I know because they told me you were coming. I don't actually know everything."

He doesn't say anything. He repositions his glasses—Calvin Klein, black, rectangular, a little hipper than he is, picked out by J. He's not comfortable with them yet. He keeps his wire rims in the bedside drawer and is planning to go back to them once he's given these a reasonable test drive.

"How are you feeling today?" he asks.

"I'm fine. Do we have to do this part?"

"What part?"

"The social part."

"You don't like to be social?"

"I find it exhausting. I'm an INFJ. The Meyers-Briggs test?"

"I know. It's in your records."

"Then why are you making me do the small-talk part?"

"We can jump in if you'd like."

"Shoot."

"Do you know why you're here?"

"Yes."

He waits.

"Why are you here?"

"I volunteered to come here."

"Why?"

"I didn't feel safe at home."

"Why?"

"You know why."

"Because of the voices?"

"I didn't call them voices."

He looks at his records. "The guides. That's what you call them?"

"That's what they call themselves. And it's not because of them, exactly."

He writes. He looks up and fools with his glasses.

"What do they look like?"

"I can't see them."

"So these aren't visions."

"They're voices."

"I thought you said they weren't."

"I said I didn't call them that. On the form. So I wondered how you knew."

"I see," he says.

"I do have visions sometimes but not of the guides. And they aren't so much voices as a presence. The voices are like my own thoughts. Except they're not."

I can hear how badly I'm explaining this. But it's not as if there's some concise way to get it across. There's not a language for it.

"Do they tell you to do things?"

"Not unless I ask. Then they only make suggestions."

"Can you describe some of the suggestions?"

I sigh. It's exhausting, talking about it. Why did I think talking about it would be a relief?

"It's small stuff usually. They'll tell me what route to take when I'm driving. What to eat. Who's calling when the phone rings. If I'm going to get a package, if someone is going to visit. If I'm getting sick and why. In fact, they don't talk that often. I have to make them talk. The rest of the time, I just get these mental images. A picture in my mind will flash and I'll know what to do."

"Can you give me an example?"

"I'm seeing Indian food right now."

"Indian food?"

"Chicken Tikka Masala. I can also smell it. It's a suggestion of what I should have for lunch."

"How do you know that's not just you wanting Indian food for lunch?"

"Because I'm not hungry and I don't really like Indian food."

"Why would they want you to have it?"

"My body needs it for some reason. There are all kinds of medicinal properties in Indian food. I've probably been exposed to a little virus."

He writes and shifts in his seat. It's not an actual squirm but it's close.

"What do you mean when you say you have to make them talk?" he asks.

"I have to be in the right kind of energetic place. I have to get rid of distractions and raise my calibrations. I usually do that through meditation but there are other ways. Sometimes if I go for a walk—if I'm in nature with not a lot of people around—the guides will just fire up. Sometimes I like it. Most of the time I like it. When they go away I miss them."

"When do they go away?"

"When I'm distracted. When my calibrations are low."

"What makes your calibrations low?"

"Distractions. Should we back up? I feel like this is not really landing."

"Well, Ms. Lange, it's a lot."

"I know. You can call me Sarah."

"I'd rather not."

"Okay, then call me Violet."

"Why?"

I shrug. "Just thrashing around for a name you might like."

He actually smiles for the first time.

"I like Sarah just fine but it works much better if we are not on a first-name basis. I'm a believer in boundaries."

"Oh, I know."

He doesn't know what to do with that. He struggles to get back on course. While he's staring at his records I blurt out, "Jennifer."

He looks up slowly. Like he doesn't want to know. But he needs to know. That's how people mostly respond to me.

"I'm sorry. I knew it was a J name. It came to me. I'm sorry. I know it's like trespassing."

"I'm not sure what you're talking about."

"Your girlfriend's name isn't Jennifer?"

Blood leaves his face and then rushes back in. He's cute red.

"I would appreciate it if you wouldn't discuss my personal life with others."

"I'm not. I'm discussing it with you."

"Ms. Lange, do you think I believe that you somehow know my girlfriend's name? You asked around."

"Asked who?"

"Anyone."

"I didn't ask anyone."

"She works here. It's common knowledge. You haven't dredged up some great secret."

"She works here?"

"On the addiction side. That's how you know her name."

"All right."

I don't tell him that we never socialize with the addicts. Sometimes we take walks in the same garden but we mostly don't like each other. I couldn't care less who drops by to see them.

But I blame myself. I know better than to blurt things out.

"Wait until asked," a therapist named Heather told me, back before I understood what was happening. I kept telling people things about themselves that I thought might help and it just agitated them and in most cases caused them to leave. "Wait until asked," she said, "and then you can tell them anything you want."

That was a great rule. I embraced it. Three weeks later I came into her office and said, "No one ever asks."

"Exactly." She smiled.

That philosophy actually worked for a long time. But now people are asking. Dr. David Sutton in particular.

"Can we get back to the spirit guides?" he asks.

"Yes."

"When did they start talking to you?"

"They've always tried to talk to me, I guess. I shut them down when it started to create problems for me."

"And when was that?"

"As a child. It terrified my parents, the things I knew. When I talked about what was happening to me, they threatened to take me to the doctor. I hated the doctor because he molested me and gave me shots."

"He molested you?"

"Later in life. I guess it was just the shots I hated."

"How did he molest you?"

"I don't want to talk about it."

"I think it's important."

"Okay, he was just a dirty old man and he asked women to take their tops off no matter what we were there to see him about. He would give us unnecessary breast exams. It's tawdry. I hate talking about it. He did it to everyone. It took me years to figure out what to call it because when I was a young girl in the South, they didn't really have molestation. It didn't have a name. It wasn't really a crime. Rape was a bad date."

"Were you also raped?"

"Look, I was raised in a small town in the South by uneducated people. There was a lot of unsavory stuff. Creepy uncles, bad doctors, dirty cops, lecherous teachers. It's what happens in a place where no one is watching. But this is not about that."

"You're the one who brought up your childhood."

"Only in relation to the voices. I had this thing where I could kind of hear people's thoughts. I had dreams that came true. I guess I was what they call clairvoyant. I think I remember seeing dead people, too. But I talked about it and it freaked everyone out and put me at risk. So I shut it down for my own survival. I didn't understand this until recently. When I started hearing from the guides again. But I don't want to go back to primordial ooze, my bad childhood, all that crap. It's a waste of time."

"There may be a connection, Ms. Lange. Between childhood trauma and your relationship with the guides."

"Like I made them up to escape my circumstances? And I'm still doing that at thirty-eight years old?"

"I want to consider everything."

"Go ahead. Do you think we could go outside so I can smoke?"

"In a moment. I'd like to make some more progress here."

From the window in this office I can see the flowers in the courtyard. I can see some addicts sitting on a bench smoking and gesturing wildly as they talk. They are talking about their disease. They are talking about how no one understands.

"So the guides began to talk to you when you were little and then you shut them down."

"Yes. I didn't know they were guides. I didn't know what they were. Just voices. Actually, it just sounds like your own thoughts until you challenge them. Then you realize these are thoughts that are being given to you. From somewhere else."

"When you say shut them down…how did you do that?"

"I don't know how to explain it. I just stopped listening. I stopped looking. And I figured out some techniques. I figured out how to leave my body."

"How?"

"Distractions."

"What kind?"

"Any kind. When I was young I would sing a song in my head and I would focus on the song and then nothing that was happening around me was happening. Later I would recite things. A sentence. A word. It's just a trick but it always worked. Then I lost control of it."

"What part?"

"The dissociation part."

"You would leave your body without meaning to?"

"Bingo."

"Are you in your body now?"

I stare at him as if he's the one who belongs in my seat. "Of course."

Be patient, the guides say. *He's not like you.*

I don't give him any sign that I'm hearing something. I know how to do that.

"Why do you say of course?" he asks.

"I'm sorry. I always think people know my interior mind."

He stares intently. "Because you know theirs."

I smile. "Occupational hazard."

He doesn't smile back.

He says, "Do you leave your body often now?"

"No. I got in trouble for it as a kid. When people see you staring at the wall like you're in a trance, or when you start sleepwalking in a chronic way, back to the doctor. So there goes that. Eventually, I got interested in boys and school and somehow that made all the mystical stuff go away. I became rooted in reality. I was just like the rest of you folks and that's where I stayed until recently."

"How recently?"

"Two years ago. I had an accident."

"What kind of accident?"

"Bad."

He waits.

"It's in my file somewhere," I say.

He writes.

"Are you afraid of the voices?" he asks.

"No. I love them."

"If they asked you to do something bad…?"

"They wouldn't."

"But if they did."

"Then I would know it was not them. And I would shut that down."

"Who would it be if it weren't them?"

"It doesn't matter. Just not them. I would ignore any negative force, anything that didn't make me feel good. It's about feeling, Dr. Sutton. An energetic experience. If something feels neutral or better, I go with it. Anything below that, I ignore."

He's writing very quickly now. I have a million things to say to him. It all wants to come tumbling out.

He's not ready.

I really want a cigarette.

Then go have a cigarette.

He won't let me.

Ask him again.

"Dr. Sutton, I'd really like to have that cigarette now."

"All right. I'm almost finished here. One more question and we'll be done for today."

"Shoot."

"If the voices don't scare you and don't ask you to do anything bad, why don't you feel safe?"

It's a good question.

"It's complicated."

"Did you think you were going to harm yourself?"

"It crossed my mind."

"Why?"

"I'm homesick."

He doesn't ask for where. He is catching on.

CHAPTER TWO

David lets himself into his small house in Venice and calls out, "Jen?" There's no answer and he's relieved. Lately, he has not wanted to see Jen for a good thirty minutes after he comes home from work. He needs to decompress. Lately, in fact, he can go longer and longer without seeing her. They don't spend every night together. She goes to her condo in Malibu for long periods of time. They don't talk about the fact that they are doing this.

He pours a scotch neat and sits on his couch and flips through his mail. Then he walks upstairs to his roof deck and stares at the wind-tossed ocean. It's gray and there are surfers in it, though they aren't catching any waves, just thrashing around. It's cold. The choppy waves look as if little bombs are going off in the water. The surfers are laughing, he imagines, at their hapless efforts.

He would like to try surfing. He pretends that he's too busy but he's really afraid of the elements and sea creatures. He's afraid of getting hurt. He's afraid. He's not sure why he insists on projecting his fears onto things when he knows that being afraid is just a state of mind and the targets are moving.

It would be more productive to admit that he is overly fearful and try to address that so he can live a bigger life. In fact, he decides he's going to do that. He's conquered fears before. He was afraid to choose psychiatry when

he was in medical school. He was afraid to ask Jen out when he first met her.
There was a time when he had an embarrassing fear of bees. He cured himself
with aversion therapy, working in a bee farm, letting them crawl all over his
face and arms. He was covered head to toe but it was still terrifying and the
fear somehow invigorated him. How hard could surfing be?

Below him, Jen is walking toward the house, her arms full of things.
Books and papers and envelopes and files. He doesn't understand why she
has so much paper. He confronts her about this sometimes.

"I'm old school," she says proudly.

"You're too young to be old school," he tells her. They are both forty.

"I'm not talking about years, David. I'm talking about being a tactile
person. I'm old school that way. The computer is alienating. I feel like it's
shouting at me."

And then he usually drops the discussion.

He lives on a walk street right off the Venice boardwalk where there are
little houses, most of them built in the thirties. His is Craftsman style. He
added the roof deck himself though it was difficult getting the permit. These
three little walk streets are really all that are left of the era when Venice Beach
had houses and quaint neighborhoods. Other than the canals, the waterfront
is nothing but apartment buildings and businesses.

His neighborhood is old school.

"Davey, I'm here," Jen calls from downstairs.

"Yes, I saw you."

"Is it nice up there? It's a little windy."

"I'll come down."

Jen has dropped her books on the kitchen table and now she is pouring
a glass of wine. "I have to work tonight," she says.

"All right."

"I almost didn't come over."

"Why did you?"

"What?" She laughs. "I missed you."

"That's nice to hear."

"I haven't seen you for three days."

"Really?"

She pinches his cheek and kisses him.

"You are such a Libra."

"How does that apply?"

"You're an air sign. You're in the air."

"Oh."

"And when you are focused on something, you lose track of time. Very Libra."

Jen is a Capricorn. He has no idea what this means but she somehow associates it with her success and uses it as an excuse whenever she's abrasive or controlling.

"So what is it?" she asks.

"What is what?"

"The thing that is making linear time disappear for you?"

"I was thinking we should surf."

"Like on the internet?"

"No, in the water."

She laughs and waits for him to laugh, too. When he doesn't she grows worried.

"Why would we do that?" she asks.

"It looks fun. I've always wanted to try it. And it would be nice to have an activity together. Other than work."

"We don't work together."

"We do a little bit. I'm consulting on a case at Oceanside right now."

"Really? My turf? Is that smart?"

"I've done it before."

"Not since we've been together."

"It's on the trauma side. We won't see each other. So what about surfing?"

"I don't know. Would cute clothes be involved?"

"Wet suits, I think."

She shrugs. "I don't know. Let me do some Googling."

"You're going to Google whether or not you want to surf?"

She laughs, then asks, "What is it, PTSD?"

"That makes me want to surf? No, I think it's curiosity."

"I'm talking about the Oceanside case."

"I was taking a stab at humor."

"Nice. But seriously, what is it?"

"I'm not sure."

"So why is she there? Assuming it's a she."

"She checked herself in."

"Suicidal ideation?"

"Yes, but it's complicated."

"She's depressed."

"Maybe. Although sometimes she's blissful."

Jen takes a long sip of wine. "Come again?"

"She claims that she has free access to bliss."

"Then what's the problem?"

"She's homesick."

"For where?"

"Heaven, I guess." He finishes his scotch and goes to pour another one.

"Oh, she's insane."

"Yes, Jen, she's insane. I'm trying to get a little more specific than that."

"Whoa. Who peed in your Cheerios?"

He hates it when she says things like who peed in your Cheerios. "No one. It's stressful. And you're mocking my work."

He wonders why he's picking a fight with her. Probably because he feels rejected over the surfing issue. It took a bit of nerve to bring it up. Then again, he knows he can't hold her accountable for his feeling that way.

"I'm not. If anything I'm mocking your clients."

"Patients. I don't like that either."

"Okay, let's change the subject."

"Yes."

"Let's talk about my clients. The drunks and the junkies."

This makes him laugh. "You're horrible. I can't believe they let you near people in any sort of pain."

"I'm a life coach not a therapist. I don't have to care about their pain. I just have to give them a game plan to get on with it."

"What about compassion?"

"These people have had too much compassion. They need structure and ass kicking. The ones who listen to me thank me later."

They've had this discussion before. That's not what's getting to him.

What's getting to him is that he feels defensive about Sarah Lange. He does not want to know what's on the other end of that.

"Look," she says, "compassion is great and that's what you're in it for. My job is about the next step. There's life beyond being understood."

"I understand."

This makes her laugh again and he loosens up. She has a musical laugh. It sounds like relief would sound if it had a tone.

"Let's make dinner," he says.

This gives Jen a lot to talk about and he turns on some music and drifts on that.

After dinner she clears the dishes off to one side and gets all of her books and noisily gets to work. David goes to his study to review his file on Allison Sarah Lange.

He opens his computer and spends a few minutes being distracted. There's so much to do before he has to get down to work, so many distractions. Email, Facebook, check the weather, news headlines, maybe a few strands of the *New York Times* crossword. Then, sometimes, he even gets distracted thinking about computers and how they work. He knows how they work. He never gets tired of thinking about it, all those electrical impulses bouncing around and the silicon conducting and not conducting at will. He even lets himself think about all the dedicated scientists who made it all come together, from Edison to Turing, and he envies their passion and even their craziness—no, that's not the right word. Not the responsible word for a psychiatrist. He envies their willingness to completely disconnect from societal norms in pursuit of something they can't even see. They were all scientists whose world view was larger than life. They were romantics in a sense. They were in love with the physical world. Turing died from eating a poisoned apple, for God's sake.

David worries that he's not in love with anything. He's a scientist in a field where everything he examines and explores is invisible, in fact does not actually exist. For all the rambling about the psyche and the unconscious mind and the ego and the superego and the id and even the conscious mind, there was no locating any of it. It's not as if it were possible to open someone's brain and point to the psyche or the ego. In this way, his field is like a quantum physicist's. No one has ever seen a particle but they have seen how they behave. No one has ever seen a person's psyche but they have seen how they behave. It's metaphor, he thinks. We all work in metaphor. Everything is metaphor, even the things that seem to be real and controlled by physical laws, because the laws themselves must be a metaphor for something else, something beyond the limitations of the optic nerve. Maybe it's as the Greeks had it. Everything is just a suggestion of what is behind it. A pale reproduction of something superior that can never be experienced because of human limitations.

But why?

He stops at why.

He thinks about how far his distractions have taken him and he recalls Sarah's repeated use of that word. Is this what she means, that distractions take you away from the moment? He jots that question down on a Post-it note.

He pulls up Allison Sarah Lange's file and scrolls through it, looking for something he might have missed.

Born in Danville, Virginia, July 14, 1975. Youngest child, middle class family, no serious illnesses or injury, no history of mental illness in the immediate family, though there is something about a paternal grandmother having had shock treatments.

In 2011 there was an accident. Patient says she was nearly killed but other than that will not discuss the accident. *See attached file.* But the file is not attached. Just a note from the admitting saying that she was treated for PTSD by a Heather Hensen, MFCC, NLP and some other letters he doesn't recognize. There are all kinds of new therapy movements that he can't (and doesn't care to) keep up with. He thinks he will call Heather Hensen tomorrow and make an appointment. As far as he can tell, Allison Sarah Lange has not had any proper medical treatment for her PTSD and he wonders who diagnosed her. He hopes it isn't a self-diagnosis or a Heather Hensen diagnosis, which amounts to the same thing.

Following the event, except for the PTSD treatment with HH, there's no evidence of her life being affected in any way. She has worked as a journalist, a copy editor, a copy writer and a technical writer. She has worked as a graphic artist. There's a common thread here. Someone with an artistic bent trying to support herself rather than some frenzied person searching for an identity.

There's no mention of marriage or children.

There's no glaring evidence, either, of mental illness.

And there's something about his own experience of her that bothers him. Her stillness. She doesn't fidget. She doesn't avert her eyes. She's completely centered, other than her sudden demands for a cigarette. She doesn't present as a mentally unstable person. She doesn't even present as a nervous person.

In fact, she makes him nervous.

Tomorrow, he will dig a little deeper at the source. As Jung says, he will take a pick ax to that.

CHAPTER THREE

I am in the courtyard smoking my morning cigarette when one of the crazies approaches me. I don't know his name. We don't all get together and bond and agree to be each other's buddies. We know that most of us aren't necessarily making sense and that the meds we're on (I am not on any, by the way) will prevent us from remembering each other's names, even if we care enough to ask. Inside the walls of a trauma ward, your concern about socializing goes right out the window. In fact, you spend a lot of time wondering why you ever bothered to connect with people and have them over to dinner and buy all that kitchen stuff. What were we all yakking about? I can barely remember. It seemed so important. Our opinions. Our views of life. We cared enough about it that we raised our voices and sometimes fights would break out. When I remember that, it seems impossible. Like it happened to someone else. But then, it did happen to someone else.

I can't remember the faces of my friends.

The crazy approaches me and he looks like Sad Jesus. He's wearing institutional clothing. This means what he came here in was not salvageable. They give those people scrubs so sometimes they look like doctors or orderlies except the scrubs are a different color and the people wearing them are obviously crazy.

Sad Jesus looks at me and says, "You could see them. Anybody could see them. They say you can't but you can. The squibs! The squibs! Go watch the film again."

"What is this?" I ask him. "JFK? Single bullet theory?"

"The squibs! The squibs!"

"Giant sea creatures?"

"Go back and look at the film. You can see the squibs going off on every floor. Bam bam bam. Going off. Exploding. Demolition style."

This sounds familiar.

"And none of the Jews showed up for work that day," he whispers.

"Oh, 9/11. Inside job."

"Just try telling people that. You know what happens?"

"Sure. They put you in here."

"But you know. You know."

"I don't know. 9/11 really isn't my thing."

"You accept their story."

"I don't think about it."

He stops and stares at me and his eyes are pinwheels. "You're CIA."

"That's right, Sad Jesus, I am CIA. You should stay away from me."

He takes a step back and then asks if I have another cigarette.

I say, "You have no idea what's in there. CIA cigarette."

"I don't care."

I give him the cigarette.

After he leaves I have a few minutes of peace. I watch the addicts strolling and gesturing at each other. I wonder what it feels like to have substances chasing and haunting you. It's such a clear-cut thing and at the same time it's so nebulous. Is it the actual drug they want or is it the addiction itself, as if they don't know who they are without something dogging them? In the absence of some kind of dramatic weakness, they'd just be people working in convenience stores or law firms. Does all of this come from our terror of sameness? Insignificance? All attention is good, even if it is negative? I know I could have the answers to these questions in a heartbeat but sometimes I enjoy my ability to question, like the old days. I like musing. Musing is a lost art. Now everyone opines. Opinions have value and people like them fast and hard.

Someone else has approached me. He has a shock of white hair, even though he is too young for it, and steely blue eyes and a placid smile that fight with each other. Maybe it's this contradiction that makes him look crazy. I wonder if I have something outward that makes me look crazy.

"Hey," he says.

"Hi."

"I see you out here."

"Yes. I come out here."

I offer him a cigarette but he shakes his head.

"So what brings you to the crazy palace?" I inquire.

"Sex addiction."

"Wow. That's a great conversation starter."

He shrugs. "You asked."

"So you're here because you like to have sex."

"Because I like to have it often and inappropriately."

"Is that the case?"

"It's what they say. In here."

"Did you check yourself in?"

"No, I was given an ultimatum by my employer."

"Who's your employer?"

"I don't want to talk about that."

"Okay."

He sits down and stares at his hands. His hands are chewed up. He's a carpenter or a musician or both and his whole story about why he's in here feels made up. I don't want to know why he's really in here so I don't ask again.

Be patient, he's not like you.

I am relieved to hear he's not like me.

"What are you here for?" he asks.

"Crazy."

"Oh, seriously? I totally took you for an addict."

"That happens, I guess."

"You don't look crazy at all."

"Thanks. I was just wondering about that."

"What's your name?" He's looking at the ground, as if that will minimize the significance, as if he won't get caught.

"I don't think we should get into that, do you?"

"Into what?"

"Knowing each other. You're a sex addict, I'm crazy, the less we connect the better."

"I guess."

He stares at the ground for another moment. My cigarette is done. I shove it into the sand ashtray. I stand up and brush off my lap but I can't remember why and then I remember it's because I used to wear nice clothes and I always smoothed the wrinkles out when I stood up. I can't remember the faces of the people I smoothed out the wrinkles for.

Whitey says, "You know you're not crazy, right? You're probably just hiding out, right?"

"Oh, no, I'm batshit. But thanks for the vote of confidence."

And I leave him sitting there, which is one of the ongoing perks of crazitude. Being able to walk away from someone not giving a shit what they think. If I ever get out of here I am taking that one with me.

CHAPTER FOUR

Heather Hensen works in an industrial complex on Wilshire, and at first David is thrown by this. He has not been imagining some business-suited Dr. Melfi from *The Sopranos*. He pictures instead a Stevie Nicks–attired intuitive with crystals and incense and pictures of Yogananda and possibly angels on the wall. Her waiting room is sparse. Industrial furniture and copies of *Time* and *Newsweek* on the coffee table. He is still contemplating which magazine to choose when the door swings open and Heather Hensen is standing there.

She is neither picture. She is a small but sturdy woman with graying blonde hair and green eyes and an open-mouthed smile that might actually be genuine. She wears a hoodie and jeans and sneakers and David is thrown anew by this. What clientele does this speak to? Who trusts this woman with her nonsensical collection of letters?

She thrusts a hand forward. "Heather Hensen."

"Dr. David Sutton."

"Dr. Sutton, please come in."

There are no angels or Yoganandas in her office. There is a non-offensive oceanscape. There's a fountain gurgling somewhere. The room smells like a spa but he can't see the source of the smells. The cabinets and desks are of some kind of oriental bent. Thai, he thinks. He cannot get a read on anything here. When she gestures, he sits on a down sofa, which cradles but doesn't swallow him. She sits across from him in what appears to be an upscale La-Z-Boy.

"How can I help you?" she asks.

He takes his laptop computer out.

"I hope you don't mind," he says, as if he's smoking. He feels the technology might offend her somehow.

"Of course not."

"I just want to pull up my files and take some notes."

"Of course," she says. She picks up a notebook from somewhere and opens it and says, "I'm old school."

He smiles.

"Yes, my girlfriend is, too."

He has no idea why he has just told her this.

"Don't get me wrong," she says. "I do use a computer. In fact, I'm a little obsessed with my computer at home. But in here, I find it's less distracting for my clients."

"Yes. I use a notebook in one-on-one sessions. Actually, my preference is not to write at all. I call on my powers of retention."

"Same here."

"But sometimes, with more complicated cases. Well, you know."

"I do."

"Let's see. You're a therapist? Analyst?"

"Cognitive Behavioral Therapy and some other goodies," she says.

"NLP?"

"Neurolinguistic Programming."

"Yes, I'm somewhat familiar."

"It's a useful tool."

"Hypnotherapy?"

"Some. It's not appropriate for everyone. So did I get the job yet?"

He looks up. She laughs. Her laugh is infectious. It sounds more like celebration than relief.

"I'm sorry," he says, "I don't mean for it to feel like an interview. I just have to get some things straight for my record."

"I thought we were going to talk about Sarah."

"Yes. Ms. Lange. I am getting to that."

"Let me know when you're there."

"All right," he says, pushing his computer aside for a moment. "Tell me how she came to you."

"Her yoga teacher referred her."

"I'm sorry. Her what?"

"Yoga teacher, Leslie."

"Leslie is also your yoga teacher, I assume?"

"God, no, I hate yoga. Leslie and I are friends from the Program."

"By which you mean AA?"

"That's correct."

He wants to write this down but knows that it will not come across well.

"And so Leslie…" He already feels at sea from the lack of surnames. But he doesn't want to go down the yoga road anyway so he changes his approach.

"Let me ask you this," he says, regrouping. "Do you know if Ms. Lange had any proper medical treatment before coming to you? Any official diagnosis? Any contact with someone like me?"

"What's someone like you?"

"A psychiatrist."

"No, not a psychiatrist. Some social workers at the hospital, she said. After the incident."

"The accident?"

"The rape."

He looks up, surprised.

"Are you referring to an incident of molestation in her childhood? By a family doctor?"

"No. I don't know anything about that."

"So when did this rape occur? Two years ago?"

Heather shifts in her chair and looks uncomfortable. "Something like that."

"Sarah refers to it as an accident."

"That probably helps her to create some distance."

"There was no record of it on her admittance form. Nothing official. Are you the person who treated her for it?"

She says, "If she hasn't told you about the rape, I feel uncomfortable going into it."

"Ms. Lange signed a release form saying we could talk to you. I assume the hospital emailed that information?"

"Yes. I received a form that seemed to be signed by her."

"Ms. Lange checked herself into Oceanside and can leave at any time. I assure you, nothing was coerced."

"I'm not saying that. I just have some questions about her mental state. If she understood what she was signing. I haven't seen her in months."

"She seems to understand what's happening to her. And obviously she wants to get better. I'm trying to help but I need more history."

Heather considers this and there's no shift in her appearance when she lets go of her defenses.

"She was raped a little over two years ago. A year, I think, before she came to me."

"Someone she knew?"

"No. Home invasion."

He takes a chance on writing some of this down and Heather watches him, her face gone neutral and moving toward tense.

"So did she seek specialized counseling?" he asks. "I mean, directly following the event."

"She did go to the Rape Treatment Center for a few weeks. She found the counseling helpful."

"Was she ever on any medication?"

"She doesn't like medication. Surely she's told you that."

"We've only had one interview."

"Sarah won't take medication."

"All right. But I guess what I'm getting at is whether or not she was ever officially diagnosed with Post Traumatic Stress Disorder."

"I don't know. Who makes that diagnosis officially?"

"Well, a psychiatrist would. Or another kind of doctor. A therapist even, but usually…"

"One more qualified than I?" she asks with a twinkle rather than an edge.

"One with some expertise in that area."

"She didn't come to me for that."

"For what?"

"PTSD. She came to me for something else."

"What?"

"A guy, initially. A bad break-up. But after a few weeks, she told me what was really going on."

"Which was?"

"I'd really rather she told you."

David sighs and fights back a sudden feeling of rage. No, not sudden. It has been lingering in the pit of his stomach since he walked in. He can feel his face turning red and he stares at his lap and begins to count until the feeling simmers down to anger and finally to a dull pulse of impatience.

When he looks up, ready to face her, he finds that she's not looking at him at all.

She is staring at a spot on the wall just above his head. He's about to turn and look when she speaks again.

"Sarah died, Dr. Sutton, during that attack in her apartment. She was choked to death. A neighbor heard the commotion and called the cops. She had no pulse when the paramedics found her. She was revived forty-some minutes after her heart stopped. That's not in your files?"

"No."

"I can't imagine why not."

"The file is just an admit form. There's nothing in it except what Ms. Lange has volunteered to tell the staff at Oceanside."

"And she left that out. Interesting."

"Forty minutes? That's medically impossible," he says.

"It wasn't forty consecutive minutes. She came and went, from what I understand."

He makes a note. He's glad she doesn't challenge him on the medical impossibility. They are still operating in the realm of normal.

"So what about that experience did she want to discuss?" he asks.

"Anything and everything. I can't go into it. I realize that Sarah signed a release form but I can't be sure she knows what she's agreeing to and I can't go into privileged information. I'm afraid that will have to be that. Doctor."

"Is that when she started hearing from spirit guides?" he asks.

Heather's eyes narrow. Somewhere in her steely expression resides a desire to laugh. He doesn't know what that laugh is about. Does she consider him stupid or lacking in imagination? Is he deprived of her understanding of another dimension?

Heather stares at the spot on the wall again, interlacing her fingers.

Finally she says, "It's safe to say that after the incident, Sarah's intuition was heightened. And it created problems for her."

"Please elaborate."

"She's energy sensitive. By nature. You do believe in energy, Doctor? Scientifically speaking. In a quantum sense."

"Of course. But that doesn't mean I think people are sensitive to it or can read it."

"She's an artist. Quite a good one. Did she tell you that?"

"No, it hasn't come up. I deduced from her files that she has some kind of artistic leaning."

"She doesn't make her living that way. Early in her life someone got to her and convinced her that all artists are crazy, and she didn't want to be that. But it's in her and I happen to believe that her denial of that is part of what's making her, for lack of a better word, crazy. You will allow that artists are often very sensitive people?"

"Yes. Of course."

"Heightened sense of awareness and all that."

"Certainly."

"And might you also grant that when people have a particular calling— excuse me, talent—and they don't allow themselves to express that talent, it can create inner conflict?"

"Yes. And I would happily get into that if it were all we were dealing with. But this woman is the victim of a violent crime, not that long ago. And before we get into trapped callings and hypersensitivity and even energy, I'd like to explore the more immediate concern of Post Traumatic Stress Disorder."

"Then you should definitely go back to your patient and do that. As we've more than adequately established, that's not my area of expertise."

She sits forward in her chair, indicating that she wants it to end here.

"Out of curiosity, what is your area of expertise?" he asks.

"Excavating the Authentic Self."

Now David wants to laugh but she beats him to it.

"I thought you might enjoy that," she says, then stands.

David is too caught off balance to do anything but follow her lead. "I'd really like to discuss this further."

"What's the point?"

"It might help me understand her."

"If you're interested in understanding her, try understanding her."

He considers pushing the matter but decides against it. Ms. Lange's near-death experience will be a useful starting point when he sees her again but he has no desire to listen to Heather Hensen's New Age interpretation of what happened in those forty minutes while his patient was dead. The rage creeps into his temple again and he thinks about all the offices and halls and avenues and nooks and crannies of unqualified self-proclaimed healers in this city, and how they send damaged people off into whole landscapes of magical thinking and superstition and, in fact, deeper and more resistant forms of their diseases. It is hard to bring people back from the angels.

He breathes and counts again and the moment passes and he closes his computer and stands. Heather Hensen has the door open already. She is equally ready to be rid of him. It is all that either of them can do to shake hands and mumble goodbye.

———•———

Since he is in the neighborhood of St. John's, David meets a colleague for lunch near the hospital. Dr. Grant Zwick is a short, dark, and handsome neurologist who got all the women in medical school. David enjoyed his company because Grant acted as bait and David wasn't a complete letdown to the runners-up. In fact, some of them later told him they'd been having trouble deciding between the two. David never quite believed them but it was believable. He was Grant's doppelganger. Blond to his dark, green eyed to his brown, and sensitive analysis of the psyche to Grant's cold, intellectual approach to the wiring of the brain.

Grant is waiting at the corner table at Drago, his favorite Italian restaurant, already working on a glass of wine and staring at his iPhone. David takes a moment to adjust to the gray taking over Grant's hair because he still remembers him as a twenty-year-old. He's certain that Grant has to adjust to David's general diminishing youth (mostly hair). Because they see each other rarely, the process is more jarring. He's not sure why they see each other rarely. They would both claim to be busy but that is not entirely it.

Grant lifts his chin and smiles and rises to give David a man hug with backslaps.

"How have you been, you bastard?" Grant says.

"Fine." David nods at the wine as he sits down. "Surgery after lunch?"

"Yes, a little glioblastoma. I like to relax before."

They laugh, physician humor.

"No, I just have lectures today. I'm not on call," Grant says, as if he doesn't trust David to understand his sarcasm. Which makes David not trust Grant's sarcasm.

He reminds himself not to analyze his friends. It's an ongoing battle.

They talk about Grant's wife, a stylist, and their recalcitrant four-year-old son Willem (probably recalcitrant because his name is Willem, David thinks, and his mother is a stylist—Korean and twenty years younger than Grant) who has been kicked out of two nursery schools. His wife is at her wit's end but Grant has a hard time taking nursery school seriously and thinks the boy is having an appropriate reaction to being indoors too much and being forced into dramatic play.

"The pendulum has swung too far, David," he says. "We've overcompensated for the girls. I'm sorry for all the years we ignored them in school but do we have to turn the boys into sissies now? My kid spends half his day at a fake stove or playing dress up."

"Not anymore," David says, trying to be light. "We don't have to compensate anymore."

"No, not anymore and not even then. That's what he was punished for. He wanted to tackle someone to the ground, not pretend to make a soufflé with Courtney and Kelsey."

"Is he into sports?"

"Very into sports. Anything with a ball. But these damn schools, they give the kids thirty minutes a day in the playground and even then, no sports, nothing with balls. Balls aren't allowed on the goddamn playground."

David chuckles and looks at the menu.

"Don't you think that's fucked up?" Grant implores.

"I'm off the clock right now."

"Not as a shrink. As a friend."

"As a shrink friend."

"Come on. Seriously."

"Seriously. Do you see me asking you about my frontal lobe?"

"Your frontal lobe seems fine. Now, tell me."

David sighs. "It would probably be helpful for him to see a child psychologist if he is having continued difficulty adjusting to social settings. Or you could supplement his schooling with league sports, give him a lot of room to compete, if it's in his nature."

"In his nature. See, that's what I'm talking about."

"Did you really need me to tell you this, Grant? You understand the brain pretty well."

He shakes his head, sipping his wine. "No, to me it's just a landscape. It's terrain. I can tell you what's next to what but it's the fucking Northwest frontier. We're Lewis and Clark. We have no idea what's going on in most of that terrain. It's wilderness, I'm telling you."

"My profession isn't? It's abstract. It's conjecture. And except in the extremes, it doesn't seem to work. Not in any consistent way."

"I've never heard you talk this way before."

"I've never heard you talk this way before."

"We're getting old, I guess."

"Speak for yourself," David says and their laughter is forced.

The waiter comes over and tells them the specials and Grant says they should have the carpaccio and the sole and David agrees and says he'll just have water when Grant orders another glass of wine.

"But back to something you said," Grant insists. "If it's in his nature. His nature. What is that? We can't find evidence of one's nature in the brain but it's undeniable, isn't it? I mean, of course it's not in the brain, it's in the DNA, the genetic coding, but it's in there, isn't it? One's nature? Such an interesting word. Anachronistic, really. But undeniable."

"It's hard to deny talents and proclivities. Hard to explain them as well. Better just to accept them."

"But a serial killer. Is that his nature?"

"This is an undergraduate discussion, Grant. I'm surprised at you."

"I feel we might have skated over some salient issues in our rush to becoming experts. Important things. Basic things that beg the question."

"Yes, we might have done that. Can we talk about the Lakers?"

"Fuck the Lakers. Kobe's an asshole."

"Then the Clippers. Anything else."

"David, you used to be up for a good debate."

"I was younger. And I knew a lot more then."

"Isn't that the truth."

There is a protracted silence. David feels guilty for dismissing his friend. Wonders if he's being an asshole and suspects he probably is. Jen would tell him he's being obstructive. Obstructive is a word they like in life coaching.

"What?" Grant asks. "You're smiling."

"I'm thinking of Jen."

"How is she? If you're still smiling when you think of her things must be good."

"I don't know about that. They are pretty much where they've always been. I was thinking of her profession. It makes me smile on occasion."

"She's a therapist, right?"

"No, she's a life coach."

"Right. That's a growing field."

"She was a professional organizer before she was a life coach. That's how I met her. She professionally organized my garage."

"Five years now?"

"Seven."

"How's your garage?"

"Disorganized."

They laugh, less forced.

"But she has a degree in psychology," David goes on. "Stanford, no less. Undergraduate. She was using her psychology degree to help people organize their lives because, she said, it was hard for people to let go. She coached them into letting go of their things. Clearing out space. She says that clutter is evidence of unmade decisions."

"That's pretty good."

"She also says that you have to make space for opportunity to find you."

"That's less good."

They laugh again.

"She was on that New-Agey spiritual side when I met her. Still is a little, if you count feng shui and smudging and the zodiac. But she works with addicts now, out at Oceanside. And she's become impatient with spiritualism."

"Thank God, right?"

David laughs at the pun.

"And she's much more into goal setting and authentic action."

"Cause and effect. Physics. Terra firma," Grant says.

"But the thing is…I don't know."

"Go on."

"She's meaner."

Grant practically guffaws. "God, what a word. Why did we ever let go of it? All of these technical terms when really, most of the time, that one will do."

"I've thought so a few times in my practice. I could say Borderline Personality Disorder with Narcissistic Tendencies or I could just say mean as hell."

They laugh loud enough that people look at them.

David clears his throat. "But of course, I don't mean that exactly," he says. "She's cranky. She has less patience with everything than when she was more… the other way."

"Flaky."

"I guess. And yet I have no patience with New Age crap. Magical thinking. You know that."

"I know that."

"On the other hand, what is life coaching about? Why should people have to be coached on how to live? It's not as if we have a lot of options. Shouldn't we just innately understand how to live?"

"Depends on what you mean by live."

"Oh, don't do that. I mean live. Engage in life. Why is it so problematic? And if you break it down, that's what my profession is about. Telling people how to live. How to get the business of living done."

"How to make the most of their lives."

"That's just semantics."

"No, it isn't."

"Of course it is. Make the most of your life. Live your best life. There's no evidence, scientific or otherwise, that that's somehow the point."

"Now you're getting into philosophy and, ah, thank God, here comes my wine. Sure you won't join me?"

"No. And I'm not talking about philosophy per se," David continues at the same speed, ignoring the waiter. "Well, not in the textbook sense. I'm talking about a career crisis. Why am I running around giving people disorders and prescribing medication? It's like I'm putting spells on them. What if we just left people alone?"

"They'd hurt themselves or others?"

"I am not talking about those people. As I said, we see success in extreme cases. I'm talking about the rest."

"The troubled well."

"Yes. Let's take you for example. Do you think your son needs medication?"

"Hell, no. I think he needs dodgeball."

"Exactly."

"But that's not PC right now."

"Exactly."

"There's no way my kid is going to be medicated."

"Good. But if you brought him to me and I didn't know you, I'd probably medicate him. Not now but in a few years. Unless you held your ground. Nobody ever holds their ground, by the way. The wife wins on this one. The wife under the spell of the teachers. The wives want their kids to fit in. Very big deal to them, fitting in. Sometimes the husband wants that, too. Fitting in. Where will the artists come from?"

Grant is staring at him. He sips his wine and gazes off.

"I'm not giving in," he says to the wall.

Mercifully, the food arrives. David feels embarrassed. He has no idea where all of this has come from. He had no idea it was in him. No, that's a lie. It's been festering somewhere, but he had no idea it was so close to the surface.

Grant asks him about his extended family and about what he's driving and about how his stocks are doing. A robust discussion of the economy finishes out the main course.

But as the waiter is pouring coffee, David says, "I haven't lost all faith in my profession. I'm just starting to have a lot of questions about it. And I'm afraid the failure to ask questions might lead to a greater failure."

Grant blows into his cup, avoiding David's eyes. He says, into the coffee, "See, at the end of the day, all shrinks are poets at heart."

It's the way he felt watching the surfers—paralyzed, stranded between inspiration and fear. Less than anything on earth does he want to be a poet at heart.

CHAPTER FIVE

D̲r. David Sutton looks tired and drained and that pink shirt isn't helping him. It brings out the red under his eyes. He hasn't been drinking or crying but it looks as if he's been drinking or crying. I am watching him cross the common room where I am engaged in an afternoon game of solitaire with real cards. I don't have an iPad anymore. They take all electronics away from you here. It's possible to earn them back over time, for private use in your room, but most people find they don't miss the constant call of their robots.

"Ms. Lange," he says. "Did you forget about our appointment?"

"No, Dr. Sutton. I assumed you would come and find me."

"It's customary to meet in my office."

"I don't like sitting in there. It feels like I'm in trouble for something."

"Well, if you'd prefer to wait for me out here, let's make that the custom."

"There you go. We have a custom."

"After you," he says, gesturing.

We go into his office, which is devoid of details, anything personal, and that is because it is a temporary office. Anyone could see that, not just an intuitive. And I know that he's not here every day. In fact, he only seems to come out here for me.

"Make yourself comfortable," he says.

"That's a tall order."

I sit on the stiff leather couch and he sits across from me in the stiff leather armchair.

"How are you today?" he asks.

"Peachy."

"I took the liberty of going to see Heather Hensen this morning."

My heart jolts. My worlds are mixing. He's into my secrets. Then I realize I gave him permission and I do not have anything to hide because my worlds finally collided and now I am in here, living one life, instead of out there, living several.

I believe the accepted definition of sanity is a shared consensus of reality. My reality was always on the fringes and because I wanted to play with the cool kids, I hid the fact that my head was basically a radio, going in and out of stations that other people couldn't pick up at all.

But here, I've admitted the truth about my head. I don't have a secret to defend. I only have the fact of it to deal with.

A picture of Heather flashes across my mind. She is laughing. Heather and I spent a great deal of time laughing even though what we were discussing was so serious. We both have gallows humor. I wonder if she and David Sutton spent any time laughing but I doubt it. She coaxed him with it in the beginning—flirted, really, because Heather is a big flirt—but he didn't go for it, he of the serious mien and the high regard for boundaries.

"How did that go?" I ask.

"It went well," he says generically.

He has taken out a notebook but he is not consulting it. His laptop sits to the side, beckoning. He ignores that, too. I know he is avoiding his routine because he worries about alienating me. Honestly. People think intuitives are so special but most of the time we are just paying attention. Paying attention to how you behave. Your behavior tells us everything.

He shifts in his seat and adjusts his glasses and says, "I'd like to talk to you about something quite difficult."

"The rape?" I ask.

He seems thrown, as if his whole game plan is derailed.

"Yes. You referred to it as an accident during the admission process. And again while discussing it with me."

"Right."

"Why did you do that?"

"Because that's what it was. I accidentally left my window unlocked. I accidentally found myself in a violent situation."

"But you understand that on the part of the violator, it wasn't an accident."

"I suppose on his part, it was an act of will. Though I have to think he accidentally picked my apartment."

David crosses his legs and leans back in his chair. I know he thinks this sitting-back posture is supposed to put me at ease. I am not at ease. I just know that we will have to discuss this sooner or later, so why not now?

I sigh and tell the story the way I tell it, as a copy writer or technical writer, explaining circumstances in an atmosphere devoid of subjectivity. It is what I am trained to do.

"Two years ago, a man climbed into an open window of my first-floor apartment and raped me and choked me and I nearly died."

"Yes," he says, as if I need him to agree.

"What do you want to know about it?"

He clears his throat and shifts. "Well, many things."

"Go."

"Well, I suppose, I wonder if you sought medical treatment."

"Yes."

"How soon after?"

"You can write if you want," I tell him.

"No, that's all right. I'm just listening right now," he says.

Like a guy who wants a drink resisting the drink.

"Tell me about your medical diagnosis," he says.

"Well, I don't remember a lot of it. The cops and the paramedics found me. Apparently I was technically dead and they revived me. More than once. Then I went to the hospital and a bunch of people treated me—not for psychological damage, just the physical thing. They kept me there for three days, making sure my heart was going to keep beating and that I didn't have any brain damage. Then the tests started. Did I have an STD, was I exposed to AIDS. Everything came back negative. I got CAT scans. I got some shots. It was a long three days. Eventually, a social worker came in to talk to me. He wore a short-sleeved dress shirt. He was about eighty. His opening gambit was, 'So I guess you're feeling pretty bad, huh?'"

David writes.

"They let me go. From the hospital. They referred me to the Rape Treatment Center. I went to counseling there. They gave me some advice on how to sleep."

"But who diagnosed you?" he demands.

"With what?"

"PTSD."

"Oh, I don't know. Somewhere in there a counselor said I had PTSD. Some kind of doctor showed up and gave me antianxiety medication. But I didn't want to take it."

"Why not?"

"I don't like to be drugged."

He writes.

"So almost two years go by," he says.

"What do you mean?"

"Almost two years where you work and function and live your life. I mean, looking at your record, you kept working."

"I find solace in work."

"I understand that. I do. But you realize that most people who endured the experience that you did might take some time off? Maybe even go away to a treatment center?"

"Like the one I'm in now?"

"Yes," he says. "But more immediately."

"Like all roads lead here so why didn't I get here sooner?"

"Something like that."

I don't know how to tell him about that. Shortly after the event, I started hearing from the guides. And I wanted to spend some time with them. I didn't want them to get drugged or shocked out of my brain. But he's not ready to hear that.

So I say, "I just wanted to get back to life. That was my strongest instinct. I spent a lot of time wandering around looking for who I was. I mean, I wasn't exactly normal before but I had a system worked out. I knew how to be in the game. It took me a while to realize I'd lost that skill."

He writes some more. He looks up. "Is there anything you want to talk about regarding the rape?"

"No. Not anymore. I kind of talked it to death. Like I said, I barely remember it. I left my body even before."

"Before what?"

"I died."

"Were you aware of dying during the attack? Or was it just something you were told?"

"Dr. Sutton, why do you do this?"

"Do what?"

"Dance around stuff. It's dishonest. Why don't you just ask me things?"

"That isn't the process. The process is to let you tell me information as you're comfortable."

"So it's okay for you to lie about what you know."

"I don't really know anything."

"What did Heather say?"

"She was reluctant to tell me anything. Although she did say that you were clinically dead, in and out, for forty minutes."

"Okay."

"And about a year later, you came to see her."

"Yes."

"Was there some reason you chose her specifically?"

"My yoga teacher Leslie recommended her."

"Recommended her for what?"

"Counseling."

"For your PTSD?"

"No. For a guy. I couldn't get over this guy. It didn't last long but it was very painful. I wanted to figure out how to move on."

"And she specializes in relationship issues?"

"I don't know if she specializes in anything. But the conversation went something like this. I was complaining to Leslie about this guy I was dating and I revealed to her that I had this kind of psychic connection to him, that when his stomach hurt mine hurt, even if we were miles apart, and that even though I was in love with him I was aware that he wasn't good for me but I couldn't put him down, like a drug. And she said, 'Oh, you should go see Heather.'"

He writes. Finally he looks up.

"So how long were you seeing this guy?"

"Not long. Weeks, months."

"So you started dating him not long after the rape?"

"About eight months. Math isn't my strong suit."

"You felt ready to pursue a relationship? Less than a year after an incident like that?"

"I don't know if I felt ready. I just met this guy and things happened."

David puts his pen and notebook down and looks at me. "I don't believe you," he says.

I stare at him for as long as I can. I want to applaud. Or stand up and walk away. Anything. I'm so nervous now that I have gone down the path of talking about this. But I am intrigued that someone cares about me enough to call me on my bullshit.

His eyes are melting me. I know I have to tell more truth.

"I really have no idea how long ago anything was. I've tried to explain that linear time doesn't work for me anymore."

"That's not what I mean," he says. "I don't believe you about the guy. That there was one or that what happened with him is important. I think it was an excuse to get back into therapy. That's fine but you don't have to keep up the ruse."

"I didn't make up the guy. But you're right, it wasn't really about him. I mean, it was and it wasn't. We met about a year after the incident, I think. I really liked him. He was handsome and smart and he made me laugh. I was struggling to be a normal person. I always wanted to be one but I really, really wanted to be one after I met him. I worked constantly and I had stopped having time for a relationship. Mainly because I hadn't met anyone who made me care enough to make it a priority. And maybe because having a man touch me was the last thing on my mind after what happened. But then I met him. And I was ready to be happy. So one night, I was sleeping over at his house. I woke up in the middle of the night with a night terror. You know what those are? They're different from nightmares. They have physical symptoms, like a heart attack. You think you're dying. It's fallout from a violent attack. That's what I learned later. Anyway, somehow I managed to have this night terror but I didn't wake him up. I went outside to his terrace.

He had this great house in the Hollywood Hills. I was sitting on his terrace, smoking a cigarette, and he came out to see about me. He asked if I was okay and for some reason, I just looked at him and said, 'I've finally met someone I want to be with but I'm too damaged. It's too late.' He didn't say anything. He just looked at me and went back in the house."

David stares at me and waits. He knows the ending but I tell him the ending anyway.

"Well, he was a guy so you can guess the rest. He never called again."

David doesn't write though I can see he wants to.

Finally he says, "Why were you too damaged?"

I shrug. "Damage is not the right word. I don't know the right word. I was beyond him."

"Because of the rape?"

"Because of everything. The rape just made it all come tumbling out. I was like this closet packed full of crap and then the door gives."

"And he made the door give?"

"And that's why I went to see Heather." I look at him and sigh. I am worn out from it all. "Look, I know how all this sounds to someone like you."

"What's someone like me?"

"A medical doctor. A scientist. An intellectual."

"How do you think it sounds to me?"

"Crazy."

"I don't use that word."

"Okay. Delusional. Closer?"

"It doesn't matter what I think of what's going on with you, Ms. Lange. What matters is treating your condition. And one of the ways that I go about doing that is by taking a history and trying to see if there's any connection between your suicidal ideation and past traumas. Since you don't seem to have any more recent traumas. Have you?"

"Not unless you consider suddenly hearing voices and having visions that you can't turn off a trauma."

"But it's not sudden, is it?" he asks. "After all, you say these visions and voices have haunted you since childhood."

"As a child I could turn them off."

"But since the event, you haven't been able to?"

I look at him. I do want him to understand. But I don't want to audition anymore. I don't want to convince anyone. The whole dilemma of this is trying to get someone, anyone, to believe that your world as you experience it is real. And then you run out of juice. You give up trying.

"Can we be done for today?" I ask. "Just check the insane box."

"Ms. Lange, I don't think you're insane. I think you might be experiencing a delusional disorder as a result of your trauma."

"Great. What about a brain tumor while we're at it?"

He puts his pad away and leans back in his chair.

"Well, I was going to have that discussion with you," he says.

"Okay."

"I know a very good neurologist at St. John's. I'd like to schedule you for a CAT scan so that we can rule out any kind of problem like that. It's a noninvasive procedure and your insurance does cover it."

"Sounds good. Like a kind of field trip."

"So you'd allow me to set that up?"

"Sure. But just so I'm not wasting your time, I don't have a brain tumor. The guides told me that. It was one of the first things they told me. Apparently, people are always mistaking them for brain tumors and they're a little tired of it."

"Well. Just to be sure."

Be patient with him. He's not like you.

"So I guess there's no real point of our continuing to talk till we rule out the tumor?" I ask.

"We can continue to talk if you'd like."

"Can I ask you some questions?"

"Certainly."

His body clenches a little when he says certainly. Mr. Boundaries isn't crazy about the idea, pardon the term, but he knows he has to give me a little bit of leeway. It's quite possible I'm the craziest person he's ever worked with. That's what I'd like to find out.

"So, what area of psychiatry do you specialize in?" I ask.

"I see cases of all kind. But I suppose you'd say I specialize in trauma."

"PTSD."

"Yes."

"And what does that usually look like?"

"It presents in all forms."

"What are the most common forms?"

"Anxiety attacks, panic attacks, with physical manifestations such as impaired breathing and heart palpitations. Secondary to these attacks, people develop agoraphobia. Hypochondria. Substance abuse problems. Night terrors, as you suggested. Loss of appetite. Depression. Personality changes. All kinds of things which interfere with life."

"Suicidal ideation?"

"Of course."

"Talking to spirits?"

"Not exactly. Sometimes people have religious conversions. Particularly when they go through the program to deal with addictions. And on occasion, people have hallucinations and delusions which eventually go away."

"With medication?"

"Sometimes. Sometimes on their own with recovery."

"So I'm not a complete freak to you."

"Not at all."

"I'm just delusional."

He smiles. It's unpredictable, what makes him smile. Sometimes he smiles out of anxiety, such as now, and sometimes he smiles because he's moved in some way. Even he doesn't know the difference.

"Well, we don't know what you are yet," he says.

"But probably not touched by an angel is what you're thinking."

"That's not in the DSM."

"There's one thing I want you to consider."

"All right."

"I don't have PTSD. I don't have any of those symptoms you described."

"But you have thoughts of suicide."

"But not because I'm unhappy."

"You're just homesick for Heaven."

Now I smile. I heard the sarcasm in his voice. It didn't leak out. It leapt out. I think he heard it too because he suddenly gets very busy with his notes.

"You were cranky with me just now, Dr. Sutton."

"I apologize."

"What's going on?"

"Nothing."

"I'm trying your nerves?"

"No. It's sometimes difficult when you argue with me."

"You're not accustomed to being argued with?"

"I am, in fact."

"But I do it in a way that is especially annoying?"

He takes his glasses off and rubs his eyes. "Ms. Lange, I apologize. This took a wrong turn when I allowed you to interrogate me. That's against procedure. It breaks one of my rules."

"You do the asking. That's the general rule?"

"Yes. And that's because often people avoid introspection by projecting their issues onto the therapist. It's an unnecessary step and one that can be avoided by having a professional policy. That way, the patient can't take it personally. Sometimes they do anyway, but that's indicative of their... situation."

"Wow. That's a big pile of therapy you just heaped on me."

He sighs.

"Ms. Lange, intellectual gymnastics is also a form of deflection. I apologize for breaking my rule and allowing us to arrive at this juncture."

"Don't apologize. I enjoyed it."

He looks at his watch. "I do think we should conclude our session for today."

"Okay."

But he doesn't stand. He sits, staring at the notebook in his lap. I wait.

He looks up and says, "So you're an artist?"

This question actually shocks me.

"No. Who told you that?"

"Heather."

"Oh. Well. Heather is one of those people who encourages. So I guess I showed her some things."

"What things?"

I shrug. Now I feel really exposed but also excited, like something is about to begin. Dr. Sutton is just looking at me, waiting for a more concrete answer.

"Some drawings," I say. "Some poems. Nonsense, really. But Heather likes things like that. She was like having a friend in a book group or a sewing circle or something. We talked about art. It wasn't really helpful."

I feel myself looking away from him. He waits, but I know my patience is stronger than his.

Finally he says, "When did you first start to think of yourself as an artist?"

I want to blurt it out. I want to say what always sits right under my skin, growling, wanting to decimate everything in sight. I don't think of myself as an artist. You don't have to think yourself into what you are. In order to live in this world, you have to will yourself into something you're not. That's what I am trying my best to do. That's what he does even better than I. That's what, I suppose, he is here to teach me.

"I try not to think of myself at all. Isn't that why I'm here?"

He stares at me with a stare I can't describe. Something between realization and denial. I don't want to look at it anymore.

He stands and I stand and he gestures me out of the room. I walk toward the common area thinking he's walking with me but when I turn around I see he's headed in the other direction without looking back.

CHAPTER SIX

On the way home from the office, David gets in a car accident.

His private practice is in a bungalow in Westwood. The buildings are modern but constructed to look like Craftsman bungalows, not unlike the one he lives in. The complex consists primarily of show-business companies. Some of his clients work in these companies. That wasn't why he set up practice there. He did it because he liked to feel at home when he worked and these bungalows reminded him of his home. The only reason he didn't actually work out of his house was fear of his clients. Privacy issues, too, but mostly fear. In his ten years of practice he has had only a few violent patients. (He doesn't call his patients clients as therapists do because he is a medical doctor and he doesn't like to sugarcoat the relationship. They are not well. He is a doctor. They are the patients.) There were a few death threats and one patient who actually brought an unloaded gun into his office. But these cases made an impression on him. He didn't want traumatized people going in and out of his home.

The reason the car accident happens is because he is preoccupied with a cutter he is treating. She is only fourteen and her name is Selena. She has two mothers but that has nothing to do with her condition. The fact that they are lesbians, that is. The mothers have everything to do with why she is cutting. One is a Narcissist, the other is probably Borderline Personality. He cannot help analyzing the parents when he treats an adolescent—it's rare when the parents aren't in some way responsible for the adolescent's self-destructive behavior. But it's tricky because the parents are also signing his checks, so he has to find a delicate way to tell them they are a big part of the problem. Not surprisingly, they never think they are a big part of the problem.

These mothers are high achievers. One is a violinist in the L.A. Philharmonic and the other is a linguistics professor at UCLA who has published many books on the subject, one of which he had actually read before he met the mothers. Their names are Dinah and Josephine. Josephine, the linguistics professor, is French. Dinah is pissed off. He can't imagine how Dinah makes anything good come out of a musical instrument. Maybe she dissociates.

They have decided that Selena is a genius and should be well rounded. She has to get a 4.0 and sing opera and play one varsity sport. Selena is managing all that. At the same time, she is painfully thin and is cutting.

Cutting has become the disorder of the decade. It is very in. So in that it's practically an epidemic. It's the new anorexia. Although the old anorexia is still going strong. He has thoughts like this. Thoughts that make him feel like he shouldn't be a working psychiatrist anymore. He supposes that he will always be one, just as priests have to be priests for the rest of their lives, even if they leave the church. They just aren't active. He should go inactive. But what would he do?

As he drives, he is thinking back to how he handled the session with the two mothers and Selena. Usually he sees Selena alone but this was a sort of update. Selena requested it. She wanted him to explain things to her mothers. But he had made very little progress with Selena because she wouldn't hold her mothers accountable for anything and wouldn't even admit that she was overextended or particularly stressed out. She didn't want to give up any of her activities. The only thing she knew for sure was that she had trouble processing stress and she used cutting as a means of doing that. She believed that they were only here to find her a healthier habit to replace cutting. That's what she wanted him to tell her mothers but he couldn't tell them that.

Instead, he explained to all of them why cutters cut. There are many reasons but the most prominent is to create physical pain to distract them from psychological pain. Cutters do not articulate it that way. Since they are extremely insistent on not feeling their emotional distress, they would never admit to having any. Instead they say that cutting themselves helps them feel pain, which is a relief since they usually feel emotionally numb, and the pain lets them know are alive. That's what the craftier ones come up with. The more honestly confused come up with nothing more profound than, "It just makes me feel better."

Selena was somewhere in between the two. She was smart and the smart are always tough. Their intellects will create elaborate mazes and you can waste elaborate amounts of time chasing them down through their defenses. It's like getting lost in Venice (the real one) at night.

He despised the French mother. Josephine. He hated her bossiness and the way she treated her daughter like a racehorse. Dinah just seemed disconnected, but dangerously so. Their dynamic bothered him tremendously. Josephine wanted what she wanted. She was a bully. She was probably a fit thrower. Everyone around her had disconnected in some way in order to submit to her, to avoid seeing her at her worst, to take care of the crazy.

Josephine was yapping at him about why she thought Selena was cutting, which was to punish her (her, not her and Dinah) and that she felt Selena's behavior was obstinate and not worthy of understanding. She didn't want the doctor coddling her (her word); instead, she wanted David to fix the behavior. To explain to Selena that she would not be able to continue at her fancy private school and go on to a fancy Ivy League college and therefore her life would not be worth living if she wouldn't stop cutting.

Neither mother seemed to mind that their daughter was dangerously thin.

During the session, Selena began to take care of Josephine.

"Maman, let Dr. Sutton talk."

"I will let him talk when I'm finished," Josephine said. Her English was perfect down to slang and idioms, but her accent was fresh off the boat.

"No, it's his office. We're on his turf, Maman," Selena calmly explained.

"I am paying for his turf. I will talk until I have made my point."

And she did.

Finally his lack of resistance wore Josephine out and she shut up abruptly.

The four of them sat in silence for a moment.

"So what are you doing to make this stop?" Josephine finally asked.

"I am going to get to what's causing it."

"It's clear what's causing it. She is trying to punish me," Josephine declared.

"Why would she do that?" David asked.

"I don't know. Why do teenagers do anything? They are ungrateful."

"I have to agree with you in one sense. I think she is doing it in part to send you a message. And that message is that she doesn't belong to you."

This actually caused Josephine's head to whip back.

"What do you mean?"

"I mean she is an autonomous human being with free will. She is temporarily in your care."

Dinah woke up briefly from some reverie and said, "Dr. Sutton, she's not adopted. Josephine carried her."

"I carried her in my womb. What do you mean she doesn't belong to me?"

"I mean you can't own people. They outlawed it."

Selena laughed abruptly.

Then the room became very quiet. Josephine was actually speechless. David felt he had accomplished the impossible and was vaguely ashamed of the satisfaction he felt. He knew what was coming next. Josephine stood up and fired him. Everyone followed her out of the room. Selena gave him a sad look but not for herself; for him. She was taking care of his feelings. She was well versed in that.

He had let Selena get away. His need to shut Josephine up surpassed his need to help a patient and that was an indication that he should probably stop seeing patients.

But what would he do?

The blank landscape of his life startles him so much he can barely catch his breath and then he is in the middle of an intersection after the light has changed and an SUV is hitting his front right bumper and spinning him around. The air bag goes off and the next thing he knows his door is open and someone is pulling him out of the car. A man in a suit with sunglasses pushed up on his head is screaming at him and he can't understand what is happening. Then the guy actually takes a swing at him and David ducks and the guy's fist hits the car and then he begins screaming again. The second swing lands somewhere on David's face and he sees stars. It occurs to him that he's never been hit before and he's fascinated by the shock of it, the cliché of the stars, and the fact that it doesn't seem to hurt.

Someone comes and pulls the guy off of him and finally he can hear what the guy is saying:

"You fucking asshole! You could have killed me, you piece of shit! Fuck you! Stay off the road, you fucking lunatic!"

David looks at his mangled Prius and at the guy's enormous Range Rover, which has a little dimple in the bumper, and he can't for the life of him understand what is happening.

CHAPTER SEVEN

I am in the dining room eating my chicken cutlet and instant mashed potatoes when I notice a very large crazy person sitting down the table from me. I don't know he's crazy from looking at him but because they make all of us eat on the trauma side. He's easily six-five with a nest of shaggy blond hair and a Kung Fu moustache of the same color. His glasses are blue and he wears a navy Communist worker's hat. From his general demeanor I can discern that he's new to this place and on a cocktail of drugs. He's still wearing that patina of shock we bring in the door with us. After a while that gives way to something else and what that is depends upon the nature of our conditions. The ragers get angrier first, then depressed. The depressed get more depressed, then angry. And so on. I went from relief to greater relief to where we find me now, feeling a tiny flicker of agitation.

The agitation began when Dr. Sutton asked me about the art. I don't know why but it feels like sand in my shoes.

Shaggy is very engaged with his plate. He's doing everything with his food except eating it. It takes me a moment to realize he's building something.

"What is that?" I ask without meaning to. The first I realize I've actually spoken is when he looks up at me.

"What?" he asks dully, as if I've just woken him up.

"What you're doing there. What is it?"

"It's called Fuck You Fuck Off."

"Nice."

I'm not hurt by his response, just surprised, and it only makes me want to stare harder. But I'm also afraid to stare harder. Then I do something inexplicable. I begin to build something out of my food, too. I make a moat with the potatoes and a bridge with the green beans over to the chicken. Then I start creating a tower out of the bread.

"Hey," he says.

I look at him. He has a powerful stare even with the drugs.

He says, "Stop playing with your food."

This makes us both burst out laughing as if we're old friends and this is an ancient inside joke.

The laughter brings a guy in white running toward us. The orderly looks at my plate and says, "Don't play with your food."

And this makes Shaggy and me laugh harder and that brings more people in white. But before I can defend us, I hear a crashing sound. I look around to see who dropped a tray, grateful to have the attention diverted, but I realize I'm the only one who's heard it. Then my ears are full of noise and suddenly I feel as if someone has punched me in the face. My head even whips back and I am dizzy.

I drop my fork and cover my ears and I know that everyone is looking at me. The dining room is usually pretty peaceful because the people who are well enough to eat in there can get very focused on eating and ignore everything around them. It's not unusual, still, for one of the Air Talkers or Hair Pullers or Face Slappers to suddenly go off and then they are gently led back to their rooms.

I have never gone off in the dining room before because, in case you haven't picked up on this, I am not actually crazy. I know exactly what's going on with me and I can control it to a degree. I am here to protect myself from doing something that I know is wrong and that I will regret. I am also here to be taken care of because when I'm with the guides, I forget to eat and sleep and bathe and things like that. It's far better to be in an environment where someone makes me do it.

Anyway, I don't have sudden tics or noticeable behaviors but the roaring in my ears is so loud I have to make it stop. It sounds like a train going through my head. Then I realize this is happening somewhere in the world to someone I know. That's how it used to work. The radio in my head would pick up the distress of someone I was particularly connected to. But I'm not connected to anyone anymore. I rifle through the files of people I used to love and I can't see them or feel them. I am about to move into the vision of it but then comes the distraction.

Christine, one of the directors of the crazy palace, has come over to me and is sitting down. She doesn't touch me because you can't touch the crazies without permission.

"Are you all right, Sarah?" she asks.

"Yes. Please leave me alone."

"You seem to be in distress."

"No. I felt faint. I'm fine now."

"Did Willie trigger you?"

"Who is Willie?"

She nods to where Shaggy was sitting. Obviously he's been led away for playing with his food and laughing too loud.

"No."

"Do you want to go back to your room?"

"No."

"Try to slow down your eating and drinking."

"I will."

She sits there for another moment to make sure I'm telling the truth.

The roaring subsides. I take my hands away from my ears and smile at her. I eat a forkful of potatoes. Satisfied, she walks away.

It's all right. It's over now.

CHAPTER EIGHT

When David gets home he finds Jen in bed with a glass of wine, wearing animal print lingerie. It disorients him and he stands in the doorway for what feels like a long time. She smiles at him and raises her glass.

"What are you doing?" he asks.

She laughs. "Well, if you have to ask it's been way too long."

He finds he can't move toward her or away.

"Why are you so late?" she asks. "This thing has been digging in to my skin for an hour."

"Something happened."

"Oh, my God, what's with your face?"

"It's a black eye. I got in a wreck."

"Oh, my God." She scrambles out of bed and he wishes she wouldn't. It's too confusing to have a woman dressed like a leopard hooker descending on him.

"Don't touch me," he says.

"I'm not going to touch you but, baby, that's some shiner. Didn't your airbag go off?"

"Yes. But that's from getting punched in the face. It's my only injury."

"By what?"

"Who. The guy who hit me."

"The guy you hit in the car then hit you in the face?"

"Yes. But I didn't hit him in the car. He hit me."

"He hit you and then he got out of the car and hit you?"

"Yes. I'm all right."

"Are you sure?"

"I went to the hospital. They did tests and took X-rays."

"And the other guy?"

"Nothing."

"Did they arrest him?"

"I don't know."

"Was he insane?"

"No. He was an asshole."

"The world is losing its mind," she says.

"Lucky for us," he says. "In terms of job security."

"Is that a joke? Are you joking?"

"I'm trying to."

"So you're okay."

"I guess."

"And the car?"

"Totaled, I imagine."

"Not a scratch on his, I suppose."

"It was a Range Rover."

She clucks her tongue. "That is the asshole car of all time. It is the cocaine of cars."

"I need to lie down."

"Do you want me to get you something?"

"No. I just want to be alone in the dark."

She watches him as he makes his way to the bed. He leans back, appreciating the feel of the bed supporting him.

"Alone?" she asks.

"Yes, if it's okay. I'm sorry about the lingerie. Can I see it another time?"

"Anytime. I just I thought we'd celebrate. I finished my book."

Jen is always finishing a book. He can't count the number of books she has written, telling people how to live their lives. Her latest is called *Stop Trying, Start Doing*. Trying is a bad word in life coaching. It is the root of all evil. It lets people off the hook. They feel they have achieved something by taking a halfhearted run at it. The world would be much better off if we'd take trying out of our vocabulary, Jen says. The Nike ad doesn't say Just Try It, now does it? And so on.

He tells her, "I can't celebrate. My head hurts. They gave me something strong. Vicodin."

"You drove home on Vicodin?"

"No. I took it when I came in. Downstairs in the kitchen. I walked up the stairs on Vicodin."

"Be careful, it's very addictive."

"Jen, I know you're just helping but you're not helping."

"Gee, it's only what I do for a living."

He sits up with some effort.

"Really? You want to do this now?" he asks.

"No. I don't. I'm sorry. I'm just disappointed. Get some rest."

He lies back down and closes his eyes and listens as she gets dressed and puts on her heels and clacks over to him. She kisses his forehead, which makes him wince from the pain, and she apologizes again. He hears her clack downstairs and then she's moving around in the kitchen gathering all her books and files.

He feels sad and remorseful and incapable of taking care of her.

"Feel better," she calls out before she slams the door.

She's a natural slammer of doors so he doesn't know if she is angry. At the moment he doesn't care.

Out of nowhere, the idea of having sex with Jen holds no appeal for him. It doesn't repulse him, just doesn't seem to have anything to do with him, as if she were a woman he would happily be friends with but would never consider sleeping with and he has no idea where that feeling, or lack of feeling, came from.

And then, lying there in the dark, he suddenly knows.

It came from meeting Sarah Lange.

CHAPTER NINE

Being in therapy with Dr. Sutton is not all of what I do here. It's not even most of what I do. That amounts to an hour once a week. Or maybe two days a week. The rest of my time is very structured but varies by day. For example, Mondays I have exercise class and arts and crafts and a few hours of free time, which is spent in a supervised setting—either the common room or the garden. We're not allowed to stay in our rooms for long periods of time. We get an hour of reading time right before bed and even then, our doors have to be open. When I say we, I mean the suicidal ones. Just plain old crazy, those people have more privacy. We've given up our right to privacy by talking openly—and in some cases, unsuccessfully trying more than once—about the Big No. Some of the therapists here actually call suicide the Big No. Meaning it's the Big No to life and it's the Big No in that it's the thing you're not allowed to do but in my case, I see it more as the Big Yes. Yes to the other side. Yes to what's more real than anything I see in front of me.

The guides agree with the therapist. They say it's not allowed. They understand the pull. They are supportive and loving as you might expect spirit guides to be. But they keep saying I have something important to do here and I am not allowed to leave. Yet they know I can't stop thinking about it, either, and that's how I ended up here. They told me about this place. They told me in that I saw it in a dream.

It was probably someone human who actually told me about it by name. Probably my friend James, a very successful television writer who goes in and out of sanity pretty regularly, the way some people go to Hawaii. He is in a loveless marriage and he goes insane instead of leaving her. He has been to several different places but likes this one the best.

I used to think that was completely self-indulgent and, well, crazy before I started hearing nonstop from the guides. I railed at him about it. I told him to get a hobby or leave his wife but to stop dropping out of life on a whim. I told him to drink. (He didn't.) I told him to do anything he needed to do but to stop using crazy like a crutch.

I smile thinking of that now.

I smile thinking of him reacting to the news that I am in here.

But he'll never know that I have come here for an entirely different reason.

I am in arts and crafts right now. I am doing decoupage. That means I'm meticulously cutting pictures out of magazines and books and trying to create a pattern, and once I've done that, I'll put them on a plate the supervisors have provided and then I'll varnish it several times and when I'm done, they'll put it on display with the others in a glass case they have in the lobby. It's like being in fifth grade. But I find the process soothing and in that way meaningful. It reminds me of my side life as an artist, the one that Dr. Sutton uncovered. I drew a little and I created palate boards for the movies I wrote and sometimes I even made storyboards that the directors would promptly ignore because they were artists themselves and they didn't want to see the picture in my head because they had pictures in their own heads. I did a little bit of work as a graphic artist but that wasn't as rewarding as fine art. It was more mechanical, less immediate, less art.

This place feels like something in between. I can make something in the neighborhood of art but I don't have to think about it too hard and travel out of my body as I used to have to do back when I was creating all the time.

But what do I mean? When was I creating all the time? Childhood, I recall. Drawing and writing poems and knowing exactly what I was supposed to do. Feeling energized and revved up, like an engine full of gas, just waiting for the open road. But then there was someone present, letting the air out of my tires. My parents telling me to stop doing that, taking my things away. They were so worried about it all. My father and mother whispering in the kitchen. Then the pressure to do well in school. Math problems and history reports. No time for creating anything. And I remember sitting in school feeling like it was some kind of prison, a death sentence. But trying to create anything made so much trouble at home. In that part of the South at that time artists were either crazy or Communist. My parents were certainly poor and their upbringings had left them with an abject terror of poverty. So the worried looks and the handwringing. The preacher coming over. Trips to the doctor. The lectures. This was not what people did. People got jobs and paid bills. People got married. People do this, people do that. As if I were not people. So I learned to hide the art along with everything else I kept hidden.

Something tells me to look up and I look up and see that Whitey, the sex addict from the garden, is in my arts and crafts class. He is sitting all the way across the room and he is staring at me but when my eyes meet his he looks down and focuses on his glue stick.

I stand and walk over and sit down beside him. He doesn't look at me.

"You aren't supposed to be in here," I say.

"Yes, I am."

"You're an addict. This is not an addict room. This is a crazy room."

"Well, I'm officially crazy now."

"What?"

"I started talking about suicide in group and now I'm in here."

"You can't do that. You can't fake crazy to get in here."

"I'm not doing that."

"Oh, really? You're suicidal?"

"No. But I'm not an addict either. I'm here because if I didn't come here this woman was going to sue me and I was going to lose my job."

"What woman?"

"I can't tell you my story here. This is art."

"This is crafts and I don't really want to hear your story."

"So why did you come over here?"

I don't know why I have come over. I don't always understand what I do.

See, the guides don't always speak. That's the problem. They don't always speak. They come and go. Sometimes the charisms fire and sometimes they don't. I have trouble controlling it. When they go away, that's when I have no idea what I'm doing, and when they come back, then I understand. When

I don't hear them it's hard to cope. Today they have been quiet and I don't know why I'm here and I'm missing my life that I don't remember and I want to pick a fight with someone. I have focused on Whitey.

He must be reading my expression (he can't read my thoughts, he's not like me, people are mostly not like me) because he says, "My name is Kit. What's yours?"

"Your name is not Kit."

"Well, technically it's Christopher. But people call me Kit."

"You let that happen?"

"I've been Kit all my life."

"You can put a stop to it."

"There's nothing wrong with Kit."

"I call you Whitey."

"Why do you do that?"

"Because your hair is white."

"Yeah, but why would you ridicule me? And why would you call me anything?"

"I don't know. Something about you bugs me."

"Thanks for your honesty."

"It's all I've got."

"Well, we have that in common."

"I disagree. You lied about why you were here," I say.

"When?"

"You told me you were an addict and you're not an addict."

"I told you what I was in here for. When I first got here, I was considering the possibility. But now I've rejected it."

"And now you're pretending to be crazy."

"I'm not pretending to be anything. I go where they tell me. I'm doing time. This is prison for me. Get it?"

"Are you a musician or a carpenter?" I ask.

"Both. Why?"

"Your hands are torn up."

"Yeah. They're getting soft, though."

"What was your job?"

"Is. I'm not fired yet. I work for a guitar company."

"You make guitars?"

"Yes, as a hobby, but that's not what I mean. Our company has factories in Europe and China and we sell them to vendors. I'm on the sales side."

"And that's the job where you sexually harassed someone."

"Well, I didn't harass her. I had sex with her. It's a long story."

"Okay, I'll hear it."

"Really?"

"Sure. I like stories. I'm a writer."

"You're a writer?"

"I was. Sort of."

"What are you now?"

"I don't know anymore."

"You're crazy."

I smile. "I'm not crazy either."

"I knew it. So you're lying, too."

"No. I'm officially crazy by their standards."

"But really you have the answers? You're a prophet? What?"

I look at my watch. "I have to go get ready for my field trip."

"Where are you going?"

"To see if I have a brain tumor."

"Oh. Well. Good luck with that."

CHAPTER TEN

David has a Prius loaner while his is in the shop. This one is black. His was silver. He feels like an imposter but he also feels dangerous, as if he's an evil genius now. He's gone to the dark side. The image makes him smile.

He feels Sarah Lange staring at him as they drive. No doubt, she is seeing into his soul or the guides are telling her something about him. He doesn't let himself wonder what that must sound like to her, what the chatter inside of her head is all about. Or if she's making it up, malingering. He doesn't think about it because, as a scientist, he is not supposed to. He is supposed to gather evidence and not make any judgment about it. The first rule of psychiatry, at least as he was taught it, was that it doesn't matter as much what he, the doctor, initially thinks is going on inside the patient's head. It matters what the patient thinks is going on inside her head. After the investigative phase, one can look at the evidence and make a diagnosis. But the rush to analyze is dangerous both to the patient and to the doctor. This does not stop doctors from doing it. The arrogant ones in particular. David struggles with snap judgments like anyone but he knows it's a weakness, not a strength. A good doctor, a good scientist, takes his time and is comfortable with not knowing. He can compartmentalize. He understands more will be revealed. A misdiagnosis in psychiatry can lead to catastrophe every bit as fast as a misdiagnosis in the emergency room. He is not going to misdiagnose Sarah Lange.

Even if he wanted to rush a diagnosis, he couldn't. He doesn't have a
handle on her. The snap judgments don't work. She is not schizophrenic.
He has all but ruled that out. She doesn't consistently present any kind of
psychosis. Post Traumatic Stress presenting as a delusional disorder is
promising but something about that doesn't sit right, either. She's too calm.
Right now, he is pulling for the brain tumor. A benign one, of course.

"Why are you staring at me?" David asks her.

"How do you know I'm staring at you?"

"I can feel it."

"So you can sense things."

"Everyone can sense things."

"Ah ha."

"To a degree."

"And what is that?"

"Part of the survival mechanism, I imagine. Fight or flight."

"But you can't qualify it."

"It's not my area."

"So you don't like to think about intuition."

"It's not that I don't like to think about it. It's just not what I do."

"But you just did it."

"That's everyday stuff. I don't address it in a larger sense."

"But how do you talk to traumatized people without discussing it?"

"I don't know. We just do. It doesn't come up. What's wrong with most of
my patients is pretty obvious. It has physical manifestations. We know why
PTSD happens. We know why its symptoms occur. It's not supernatural. It's
physiological."

"Got it."

"You didn't answer my question."

"What was it?"

"Why are you looking at me?" he asks again.

"Because you have a big black eye."

"I was in a car accident."

"Oh," she says. Then, "Oh, now I get it."

"Get what?"

She's quiet for a moment.

"The black eye," she finally says.

"I don't think that's what you meant."

"I don't want to talk about it anymore."

"All right."

He can tell without looking that she has turned her head toward the window and is staring out. How can he tell that? He glances over. He is right. It's a good question. How do people sense other people's movements? He has never cared about that question before. He resists caring about it now.

"Are you okay?" she asks.

"What do you mean?"

"After the accident. Is that all that happened? The black eye? No concussion or anything?"

"No. They checked for that."

"Was it your fault?"

"No. Maybe. I might have run a light. I'm not entirely sure what happened. I was preoccupied."

"With what?"

"Work."

"Not me."

"No, as a matter of fact, not you. Another patient."

"I'm jealous."

"Why?"

"I want to be the person who got you into an accident." She laughs. He realizes he doesn't hear her laugh much. Maybe he has never heard it. Maybe he has and hasn't paid attention.

"I'm sorry to disappoint you."

"Maybe next time."

Now he laughs.

"So what if I don't have a brain tumor? What happens then?" she asks.

"I don't know. Let's just rule out the neurological implications."

She looks out the window again. "I've forgotten what L.A. looks like. Sometimes out there in Malibu I start to think I'm in Greece or somewhere."

"Have you been to Greece?"

"Yes. I spent some time there with my ex-fiancé."

"You were engaged?"

"Yes."

"That wasn't on the admit form."

"I didn't want to get into it."

"Are there other big things we should know?" he asks, trying to sound casual.

"That's not a big thing. I was engaged for several years to an Englishman. Then I got un-engaged."

"Children?"

"No. That would be a big thing."

"After we rule out the brain tumor, we should go over your history again."

"That's going to be really boring."

"I'll be the judge of that."

"Listen, David, I mean Dr. Sutton, the past is not what any of this is about."

"I'll be the judge of that, too."

She sighs. "How do you do it? How do you give yourself permission to determine how another person's mind works?"

He drives, concentrating on the traffic. Finally he says, "People are in pain. They ask for help."

"Sometimes. Sometimes you just impose help on them."

"Not in your case."

"Look, I wanted to be in a controlled environment. But I didn't want people rummaging around in my mind. I have to submit to it because those are the rules. I am not happy about it."

"If you are afraid of what you might do when you are unsupervised, you need help. Your thinking is disorganized. There's a reason for that. And there's a solution to it."

"Wow. That's how it works in your world."

"Yes."

He can feel her thinking about it. He doesn't want to feel her doing things. It makes him squirm.

He says, "Let me ask you something. Don't you have friends? Family? Somewhere else to go?"

"No."

"Why not?"

"I had all that once. Little by little it went away."

"After the accident?"

"It started before then. Then it picked up speed."

"Because of the accident?"

"Yes. People don't like damaged people. Unless they are also damaged. I hung with the competent crowd."

"But you say it was starting to happen before the accident. Your drifting from people."

"They drifted from me."

"Why?"

"I think I was becoming uninteresting. I was losing interest in myself, anyway."

"Why?"

"Because I was uninteresting. We're approaching a hall of mirrors, here."

"Do you think you came to Oceanside to be with damaged people?" he asks.

He sees her thinking about it. He swears he can feel her thinking about it.

"I don't know," she says. "Maybe it's just a brain tumor."

They don't talk anymore until they're inside St. John's. Grant Zwick meets them in the exam room and introduces himself to Sarah and a nurse takes her away and gets her ready for the CAT scan.

"Wow, she's something," Grant says.

"What do you mean?" David asks.

"What do I mean? She's gorgeous. You haven't noticed that?"

"She's pretty. A lot of women are pretty. Actually, she's not that pretty. She's just interesting."

"Yeah. Interesting in a way that makes me want to leave my wife."

"Don't be an asshole. A couple of drinks make you want to leave your wife."

"Does Jen know you're seeing her?"

"Jen treats famous actors. We don't police each other that way. Besides, what am I saying? She's a patient."

"What is it about her?" Grant asks. "Her eyes? There's something about her."

"Never mind. Pay attention to her brain."

After Sarah is loaded into the machine, he stands behind Grant and watches as her brain comes up on the screen. Somehow, it embarrasses him. It feels intimate. He is looking at her brain. A part of him expected it to look different somehow, magical even. But it's just a brain. And even to his relatively untrained eye, he can see that there are no abnormalities.

"That's one good-looking brain," Grant says.

CHAPTER ELEVEN

Out by the rose garden, Kit tells me his story.

It's a tawdry tale of a rich man who hired him to run the sales department of his guitar company and then he found out he was actually reporting to the man's nephew who was only twenty-six, inexperienced, and deeply threatened by Kit. Kit and the nephew got along on the surface but clashed on a deeper level, and it culminated in the two of them both falling for the receptionist who was in her early twenties with a nose ring (he added this detail to make it clear that she seemed much older), and Kit won this competition and he and the receptionist went out for a while. Then the nephew talked her into accusing Kit of sexual harassment and she agreed and it was reported upstairs to the rich guy uncle and he told Kit that he could still have his job if he'd apologize and seek treatment for his sexual addiction. So here he is. When he's done with his tale he extends his arms, palms to the heavens, and waits for me to be—something—exasperated?

"Is he paying for this?" I ask. "The rich boss?"

"Yes. Well, my insurance is but it's his insurance."

"So he must believe in you."

"You're missing the point."

"The point is that the nephew tricked everybody and won?"

"Sort of. There's more."

Oh, God, there's more. I don't say this.

The rich boss, he says, is so cheap that he cooks the books so he can avoid giving the salespeople the commissions they deserve. The nephew does this, too. In fact, a week or so before he was accused of sexual harassment, Kit had taken it up with his baby boss that his paycheck was a little light, and there was an argument and the next thing he knew, he was here.

"Did you like her?" I ask.

"Who?"

"The receptionist. Ms. Nose Ring."

"Sure."

"You were still seeing her when she charged you with sexual harassment?"

"No, it was over by then."

"How long did it go on?"

He shrugs. "Three weeks."

"You both decided it was over?"

"I don't know. I stopped calling. She didn't seem to mind. There wasn't much future in it. Especially when I realized how old she was."

"How old was she?"

"Twenty-one."

"So, that might have had something to do with it. Rejecting her, that is."

"I don't know. All I know is I went out with a girl a few times and suddenly I'm accused of being an addict and crazy. Meanwhile, the people who set it all up, and who cook the books and cheat people right and left, they get to stay out in the world and be sane."

"That sounds about right," I say.

"How is that right?"

"I didn't say it was right. Just sounds like the world to me."

"The good guys lose?"

"No. I don't see things that way. Pairs of opposites. Good and bad, right and wrong. Linear dualism. But that's how everybody else does it. And in that world it does seem like the cheaters win a lot."

"Everybody else?" he asks. "What do you mean?"

"I have a different worldview, Kit. I'm crazy. Remember?"

"You don't seem crazy to me."

"Yet you're looking at me like I'm crazy."

"No. I'm looking at you like you're wrong."

"Okay."

We are quiet for a minute. I think about lighting another cigarette but I'm afraid it will look like an invitation for him to stay. I don't mind his company, which is to say I don't mind his energy, but his talk is fraught with negativity and dishonest.

"So I take it you didn't like my story," he says.

"No, I think it's a good story. It's got everything. Absent king, evil prince, evil princess, exiled warrior, everything but a dragon. Is there a dragon?"

"Not yet," he says. "Being crazy might be the dragon."

"But you're not crazy."

"Not yet."

I smile.

"Hey," he says. "Is that your doctor?"

I look up and see Dr. Sutton entering the courtyard. He is annoyed. It is not in his face because his face is always a poker face. It's in his shoulders, which are creeping up toward his ears, and in the death grip he has on his briefcase.

"Oh," I say, standing, "I lost track of time."

The doctor approaches me with severe intention.

"We had an agreement, I believe?" he says.

"Well, we have a custom. Which is less binding than an agreement, I believe. But I lost track of time."

He doesn't say anything to that.

"This is Kit," I say, indicating. "He's an addict and possibly crazy."

Dr. Sutton nods at him, then makes a gesture for me to follow him. I turn and give Kit a little shudder and he laughs.

Dr. Sutton doesn't talk to me as we walk to his office. Once inside, he takes a moment to get situated before he even looks at me.

"How are you?" I ask.

"Fine. Thank you."

"Me, too."

He gets out a notebook and a pen.

"Do I have a brain tumor?"

He looks up. "You do not. Dr. Zwick showed you the results."

"But you're acting like I might have a brain tumor."

"I'm trying to consider how we can proceed in a more organized fashion."

"All right."

"Because now that we've ruled out any medical condition, I'm going to take a full history from you and that can be challenging unless we establish strong boundaries."

"You keep talking about boundaries. Are you worried about crossing them?"

"Ms. Lange, we are going to discuss intimate details of your life."

"We are?"

"If we are going to get to the bottom of what's troubling you."

"Nothing is troubling me other than the suicide thing."

"That's a pretty big thing."

"So everybody says."

He writes.

"The first thing I'd like is a consistent history. For example, I had no idea you had been engaged."

"I was engaged for five years. His name was Benjamen Gold. He was English. He's still English. He's also Jewish, though not devout. Unless he's changed. He went back to England after we broke up. We don't talk."

"When did this breakup occur in relation to the accident?" he asks.

"We don't have to call it an accident anymore. I know you're doing that to make me feel more comfortable."

"All right. When did this happen in relation to the attack?"

"A couple of years before."

"Around the time you started to feel uninteresting?"

"I guess."

"What did he do for a living?"

"He was an investment banker."

"An odd choice for an artist."

"I wasn't an artist when I met him. I was a technical writer then, I think. I wrote a training manual for his bank. That's how we met."

"And why did you break up?"

"I don't know. We ran out of juice. We both cheated. It just died."

"Would you say you were depressed after that?"

I think about it. I'm not sure what people are talking about when they use that word.

"I have always felt mildly disconnected," I say. "If that's what you mean."

"Did that feeling escalate after he left?"

"I guess. In a gradual way. I let my work slide a bit. I was living hand to mouth. That was unusual for me."

"So you lost your ambition."

I laugh. "It's a little ambitious to call what I had ambition. I had a work ethic, maybe. I guess the best word to describe myself around that time was lazy. I didn't do more than I had to."

"You stopped caring about yourself?"

I look at him. For some reason, that sentence sounds incredibly odd. And a little alarming. As if it might mean something. I'm sure other people have said something like this to me before but this is the first time it sounds like something other than phraseology.

"I stopped caring about myself," I repeat. "So I accidentally left my window open."

David flushes. "No. I'm not saying that."

"I'm saying that."

"Don't say that. You weren't attacked because you left your window open."

"I wasn't?"

"You were attacked because you had the misfortune to be in the path of a violent person."

"So it was random."

"Yes."

"Even though Freud says there are no accidents."

"That's an oversimplification of what Freud said."

"I believe it's exactly what Freud said."

"I'm more influenced by Jung."

"Serendipity then. Whatever way you turn, patterns, mandalas, meaning. How do you make random work? You use it to fill in the blanks?"

He flushes. "I believe we are getting off course."

"I want to know how things work in your world," I say.

"What is my world?"

"Mechanistic."

"What does that mean?"

"Cause and effect. Linear time."

"And that is not your world?"

"Sometimes it is. It comes and goes."

"What comes and goes?"

"I can't explain it. The way I move back and forth. Some days I can't glimpse it at all. I just remember it."

"Remember what?"

I sigh. "The quantum side. The way things really are."

He doesn't write. He just stares at me with his penetrating green eyes. They are the same color as mine but I think mine are dreamier, less intense.

He doesn't write. He says, "So to go back to the event, you see no correlation. Between your breakup and losing interest in yourself."

Suddenly I can see something, like a landscape, or a mandala, or a tapestry, or a helix, or whatever the perfect word is to describe patterns falling into place. I know I am being allowed to see this. I just don't understand it entirely.

I take a moment to figure out my wording.

"I was getting lost," I say.

"I don't understand."

"I was losing myself."

"When? After the breakup?"

"All my life. And then..."

He waits. "Then what?"

I look at him. "Then I left the window open."

He stares at me and I can see a coldness creeping into him. He is hardening before my eyes, like watching something freeze.

"So God sent you a tragic event to get your attention?" he asks. The sarcasm isn't remotely disguised. It's uncomfortable, as if I've watched him dribble on his shirt or drop his pants.

"Wow, Dr. Sutton," I laugh. "That is one giant leap for mankind right there. Not very professional, all that dripping disdain."

"I apologize. Let me rephrase it. Do you think this event occurred as a kind of message or warning?"

"No," I say.

He doesn't believe me. He waits.

"I think it's a problem if you're blaming yourself," he says.

"I didn't say that I blamed myself."

"You don't bear any responsibility."

"Okay."

He writes and then looks at me and I can feel that we've hit a stalemate. I feel more than that. I feel some strange kind of anger directed toward me. The energy inside his chest looks like an electrical storm. I don't understand it. He doesn't, either. He takes a few deep breaths and the energy calms down.

"Can we talk about an earlier time?" he asks.

"God, tell me you don't need to go back to my gothic Southern childhood."

"It might be helpful."

"Well, it was gothic. Histrionic women, men with their secret lives, lots of yelling but also lots of laughing and really good food. Can we leave it at that?"

"Any abuse?" he asks, getting back on track.

"Nothing special."

"Run-of-the-mill abuse?"

"You got it."

"You mentioned that your parents were opposed to your being an artist. When did this begin?"

"High school, I guess. But I scared them a long time before that."

He writes.

"Dr. Sutton, can we talk about what's really going on?"

"What is that?"

"You are afraid to hear my story."

"I'm trying to do that."

"No. The real story. What happened after the event. What's happening now."

"The guides."

"Yes."

"We're getting there."

"I don't think we are. I think we're avoiding it."

"Ms. Lange, I promise, we will get there. But in my mechanistic, cause-and-effect world, every aspect of a person's life is connected. It's all interwoven and cannot be compartmentalized. It's a continuum, if you will."

"I will if you will."

He doesn't smile. "There is no way to separate what's happening with you now from what happened to you as a child and as a young adult and so on."

"I get it."

He leans forward. "Why do I get the feeling that you are humoring me?"

"I don't know. I didn't think you got feelings like that."

"Okay. Why am I picking up in your body language and the tone of your voice that you are humoring me?"

"Because I'm humoring you."

"Why are you doing that?"

"Because you're not ready."

"Ready?"

I nod.

"So that's your job? To take care of the therapist?"

I swallow and breathe through my nose and listen to the silence to see if I can pick up on them.

Just tell him.

"I'm afraid of your anger," I say.

This actually causes his head to jerk. Then he sits back in his chair.

"I'm sorry. I didn't realize you felt that way. I'm not angry."

"My mistake."

But we both know I am not mistaken.

He doesn't write this down.

CHAPTER TWELVE

Dinner with his family makes David feel small and cheap. No, worse than that. Learning disabled. Autistic. He feels they see him this way, too. He knows it might be projection but sometimes things are what they seem.

It is a house full of doctors. His father is an internist, his mother is a gynecologist, his brother is an orthopedic surgeon, his sister is a family practitioner, which is the latest generation of internist. To them, he is out of the circle. He's a bit of a witch doctor. People's psyches aren't of interest, because they are completely outside of the vessel, the physical form, the machine—the only thing that is, in fact, real for his family.

His older brother is a poser. He loved sports in high school but was a terrible athlete. This is his way of hanging out with jocks. No, more than that. This is his way of controlling them, becoming God for them. They made fun of him in high school; now they can't make a move without him. He tells stories about the Lakers and the Dodgers and the Clippers whom he's gotten to know—names that mean very little to David, but admitting that would put him even deeper in the dunce's corner.

Rich Sutton is very preoccupied with his status. He wears expensive clothes and has an expensive haircut and a spray tan, and a little bit of work has been done around the eyes and chin. He drives a Ferrari. His wife, Sherry, seems to despise him but she never has to see him and they probably have some kind of understanding. They are in love with their lifestyle, not each other, and as long as that is maintained, the pH of the relationship is balanced. David realizes that he's this hard on his brother now because as a kid, he idolized him. There is nothing so difficult to bear as a fallen hero.

Greta, his younger sister, dances for their parents' approval. Every time they get together she has another story about some amazing diagnosis she made against everyone's protestations. She has a perky face and a gymnast's body but she has been unable to settle down with a man. She cycled through underemployed men until she got tired of picking up the check. Then she began cycling through married surgeons, which is where she is now. A married plastic surgeon, no less. Their parents don't know this. She's sure he's going to leave his wife. She's so sure of it that she hints at their relationship to their parents, which makes David nervous. He knows it won't be well received. He knows Greta will have a mild breakdown in the face of her parents' disapproval. Whenever he sees her leaning toward this path, he interrupts with meaningless conversation.

He tries not to talk about his practice. On the rare occasions when he does, he only gets a few sentences in before his father starts questioning the hard science of his profession. Then he'll say that doctors of his kind are pharmacists. They make a diagnosis of the disorder of the week and dispense drugs. No matter how much David tries to protest, he looks guilty. He is on the conservative side of the drug debate. He prefers not to prescribe unless absolutely necessary. But the patients demand it and sometimes he capitulates to avoid losing their business. He tells himself he is worried about their psychological pain, and he is, but he's also worried about their business.

The problem with discussing his job lately is that he has started to feel the way his father does. He knows he got into this profession out of a genuine desire to help people in pain. He knows that he still does that and is driven by that. But the profession itself has changed so quickly and so comprehensively that he has scarcely had time to keep up with his motivations. Resisting the pharmaceutical remedy feels like trying to resist the Beatles in the '60s or, more accurately, McCarthyism in the '50s. But does the holistic approach work much better? Does the talking cure liberate anyone or just make them addicted to talking? He worries that they begin to fall in love or at least identify with their conditions so completely that giving them up would be tantamount to death. Every breakthrough seems to lead to another buried problem and even he doesn't know what's at the end of the rainbow anymore. Life is difficult. This is the thing he cannot cure.

The dinner is on a Sunday night at his parents' house in Holmby Hills. This is not where he grew up. As a child they lived in a small house in a nondescript area of Westwood and his parents worked at UCLA. It wasn't until later in life that they became interested in money and both went into private practice. When the kids were all gone, his parents finally purchased the kind of house one would fill with children. They say they are waiting for grandchildren. David feels that perhaps it's something else, that they didn't want a home their children might mess up, and now they have the luxury of living in the style to which they dreamed of becoming accustomed.

The dining room is large and ornate, full of heavy dark furniture and candelabras and mirrors and gilded frames. They have a cook now. They are served around the table. It feels like a Merchant Ivory movie.

The meal is cassoulet and David has his work cut out for him, extracting the foods he does and doesn't like from the concoction. He has learned to do this surreptitiously so his family doesn't make fun of him. Rich is droning on about a baseball player's rotator cuff and David is grateful for the filler.

"Where's Jen?" Greta suddenly asks.

It takes him a moment to realize she's talking to him.

"Oh. She's working, I think."

"On a Sunday?"

"She does her prep work on Sundays."

"What is her prep work?" his father asks.

"I don't know. We don't talk about the specifics of our work that much."

"Why not?" he asks.

"Donnie, they can't," David's mother, Verna, says.

"Why not?"

"Because of patient confidentiality," she says.

"They don't have to get specific."

"That's not the only reason," David says. "I just like to leave work at the office. I want to talk to Jen about other things."

"What things?" Rich asks.

Sherry looks up with interest. She waits.

"We like to cook. We talk about cooking. We talk about the book she's writing. That's not really like work. We talk about vacations we want to go on. Camping, we like that. Lately we've talked about surfing."

"Surfing?" his mother asks with alarm, as if he's talking about joining a cult.

"Stop, I'm getting depressed," his father says and everyone laughs.

"Why is that depressing?" David challenges.

"Well, David, what's it about?"

"It's about our interests. Things we are interested in."

"Not very intellectually stimulating."

"Not everything has to be intellectually stimulating."

"Well," his father says, and leaves it at that.

"We sometimes talk about politics," David pipes up and he feels like Greta, chasing his father's approval.

"What about them?" Rich asks.

Sherry has gone back to eating, seeing that none of this is going to help her relationship.

"Just what's going on, what the ramifications are."

"Is she liberal?" Greta asks.

"As far as it goes."

"What does that mean?"

"We take a measured approach. It's not a passionate debate. It's a discussion."

"Don't you want to have a passionate debate?" Greta insists.

"No. I find that getting angry about politics is just a deflection. An avoidance."

Unwittingly, he has wandered into his world.

"How is that?" his father asks.

"All of that bile and vitriol, it has nothing do with politics," David keeps going. "It's just rage. Rage always has a moving target."

"What do you mean, darling?" his mother asks, as if he has stopped making sense and it concerns her.

"I mean, Mother, how can anyone get that worked up about health care? They can't. It's just a replacement. All rage, which is unexpressed hurt, is rooted in the childhood. It is an immature emotion. It moves around because the person does not feel safe to place the anger where it belongs."

"And where is that?"

"The father, usually," he says. He's tired of it. He has found his nerve.

"Your father?" his mother asks, turning pale.

"Not my father. The father. The father figure."

"Why the father?" his father asks.

"Because rage is associated with violence. Violence is most often associated with men."

"Don't women feel rage?" his father asks and it almost seems like genuine interest.

David feels irrationally encouraged, as if he's never kicked this football before.

"Of course they do, but it's socially unacceptable in women. So they learn to decompensate in different ways. Women are allowed to cry, so that's a form of releasing rage. In many ways, it makes them the healthier of the genders, which is probably why they live longer."

"Interesting," his father says, then gives his wife a furtive wink.

David feels the very rage he is talking about building somewhere at the base of his skull.

"My goodness," his mother says.

"You two act like you're hearing this for the first time," Rich says. "Like you stopped reading medical journals somewhere around the turn of the century."

"I probably did stop reading them around then," his father says.

"Not this century, Dad," Rich says.

David is surprised and moved to witness his brother's defending him. The rage dissipates and he's overcome by a desire to ask his brother to go to a ballgame. He doesn't really follow sports anymore so the kind of game doesn't matter. Any kind of game involving a ball.

"It's just always a bit surprising," his mother says. "I spent all my days trying to get healthy babies born into the world. We probably neglected what the women were going through emotionally. We probably forgot the women were doing anything but carrying the babies."

"Yes," David says, "you probably did."

He says it without rancor because he feels none but he can see that his mother is hurt. He feels the judgment in his father's eyes now. He doesn't know how to talk to them. He, who specializes in talking.

He pictures himself standing up and pulling the tablecloth off the table, leaving the dishes intact, magician style. Or better yet, he pictures himself dematerializing.

"I think he's right," Sherry says.

Everyone looks at her. Her collagen lips seem to be quivering a little.

"Right about what, darling?" Rich asks.

"No one cares about how women feel."

"I don't think that's what he said. That's not what you said, is it, bro?" Rich asks.

David doesn't know if that's what he said. He doesn't know why Rich is calling him bro, which he's never done. Maybe it's how sports people talk to each other. He looks at his plate. He has devoured the cassoulet and can't see anything left that he wants to eat.

"Daddy," Greta says. "Did I tell you I diagnosed a case of scarlet fever this week?"

"What the hell?" he says. "I haven't seen that since medical school."

"I know."

"Are you sure?"

"I referred him to an infectious disease doc. Labs came back positive."

"How did you come up with that?"

"Strep is going around."

"But it rarely presents that way."

She shrugs. "I just knew."

"That's my girl."

The chitchat goes back to things that make them all comfortable.

David wonders how the evening would shift if he suddenly said, "Hey, did I tell you I am treating someone who hears from spirit guides? That's right. Invisible guides talk to her. She has a foot on the other side. She's able to tell us what God thinks. Do I think she's crazy? Well, of course I think she's suffering some kind of delusion, but certifiably insane? No, I don't think she is. How do I explain this? I don't. And sometimes, I don't even want to explain it. I just want to let it be."

It scares him how much he wants to say it.

It scares him even more how much he is starting to believe it.

CHAPTER THIRTEEN

I officially meet Shaggy in sewing class.

I have been percolating on the gentle giant for a while now. Since the incident in the dining room I have noticed him lumbering around the courtyard. Other than my decision that he is an artist—a judgment I made when I witnessed him building cities out of his food—I haven't come up with much except that he's definitely having trouble reining in his brain.

He doesn't talk to anyone, ever, that I can see. He stares at the ground a lot and smokes. When he's in the common room, he stares at the television as if he's not really seeing what's there. Sometimes he stares at the middle distance as if he's seeing spirits. Nothing alarms him or even seems to register until something gets loud. If someone yells or something falls to the ground his attention is immediately snared and his face turns red and he looks as if he might kill the source of the sound with his bare hands. The most he ever says about it is, "Hey!" Because when the noisemakers see who is disturbed, they don't want to make a thing about it.

Shaggy enjoys sewing class. He's meticulous about it. We have our choice of hand or machine sewing. The class offers crocheting, knitting, embroidery, quilting, pillow or clothes construction for those able to concentrate at that level. There are only a couple of people who want to go near the machines and I figure they are already sewers in life and it is second nature to them. One thing about being crazy, it doesn't inspire one to venture across new horizons. Familiarity is what they want. Busywork. I myself am not afraid of learning anything new, I just struggle with the point of it. I don't know how much longer I'm going to have to be here. Not here, crazy palace, but here, on earth.

Shaggy is doing some kind of fancy overlay. Something between quilting and embroidery. He is stenciling designs, then cutting the fabric up into little pieces and sewing them on a larger piece of fabric. I want to take a look at it but I have a feeling he won't like that. I concentrate on my crocheting and after a few minutes I'm surprised to see him lumbering in my direction.

He can't know your interior mind.

"Can I have some yarn?" he asks. His voice is low and soft.

He doesn't remember me but why would he remember me?

"Excuse me?"

"I need yarn," he says flatly.

"Oh. There's some on the table."

"I need yours."

"Oh?"

He pauses and scratches his head, which makes his blond hair stand up.

"I need it for blood," he says.

"I'm sorry?"

He seems frustrated. He gathers his thoughts, then tries again.

"I want to make blood on my design and you have all the red."

I look down and see that I do indeed have a generous amount of yarn in the neighborhood of red. I would call it maroon but I don't want to get into it with him.

"Okay. Take it all," I say, handing him a skein.

"I don't want it all. Just a foot or so."

"It's easier if you just take it."

"Are you sure?"

"Yes. I'm bored with this color. I want to switch."

"I hate to take your yarn."

"Don't worry about it."

He takes it and starts away, then comes back. "I'm Willie."

"I'm Sarah."

"Thanks, Sarah."

"Do you mind if I come look at your design?"

"What?"

"I'm interested in what you're making."

"Oh. Okay."

I follow him as he lumbers back to the small round table where he was sitting. When he sits at the table he looks like a huge boy being punished in school. But he doesn't sit now. He stands towering over his piece of art, which is carefully spread across the table. Somehow he has created an abstract design of a shark eating a woman. But it's not scary or macabre or even funny. It's strangely beautiful. I can't stop looking at it.

"See, I need the blood," he says.

I watch as he takes the yarn and creates a stream of blood from the shark's mouth all the way to the end of the landscape, a single strand, like a signature.

"Wow," I say.

"Yeah?"

"Yeah."

"Do you think my wife will like it?"

I laugh. "I don't know. Does your wife have a sense of the absurd?"

"Absolutely."

We stare at it for another minute.

"Hey, thanks again for the blood," he says.

"Happy to help."

He pans across the room. "Hey, do you feel like having a cigarette?" he asks.

"Yes. But we have ten more minutes of sewing."

"Oh, it's okay. Janice always lets me leave."

I look at our sewing supervisor, an intense, wiry woman who knits like her life and those of several others depend upon it. Her needles fly and clatter and she rarely lifts her eyes.

"Hey, Janice," Willie says in his soft, low tone. She looks up as if she is tuned only to the frequency of his voice.

He makes a smoking gesture.

She looks at the clock, then shrugs and nods.

He points to me, indicating that he's taking me with him.

This makes her sigh and shrug. But she doesn't object.

Outside in the courtyard while we are smoking my cigarettes—he has run out and is forced to pilfer until his wife comes to visit—he talks a little about how much he hates it here and how he is looking forward to getting out. The first thing he's going to do is go surfing.

"Oh, you surf?"

His face changes and his eyes roam the ground as if he's dropped something.

"Wait," he says. "Oh, shit. I can't surf anymore. I think."

"Why not?"

"I broke my elbow snowboarding. I have pins in it. They say I can't surf for a year. But maybe it's been a year. I don't know."

I don't say anything. I just wait.

"I have trouble remembering things," he says.

I nod.

"I had a treatment yesterday. Or two days ago."

"What kind of treatment?"

"ECT."

"Shock treatment?"

He nods.

"They do that here?"

He shakes his head. "I have to go somewhere. It's a hospital near here. Or maybe it's far. My wife takes me."

"I see. Does it hurt?"

"No, they put you out."

"That's good."

"But later it hurts a little. Your teeth hurt. Because you clench them. I broke a couple. And you have a headache. And you can't remember anything."

"When does your memory come back?"

"Long-term memory, I usually have some access to that. It's strange. It's like a tapestry with holes in it. Some things are very clear. Some things are just gone. I don't have any short-term memory for about a week after it happens."

"Is that the point?"

"Is what the point?"

"Forgetting."

"No. I don't think so. I think the point is rewiring. No, what do they call it? Resetting. It's like a reset button."

"Is it?"

"Not exactly."

We smoke in silence. It takes a long time for him to come back from wherever he's gone.

"Hey, what are you in here for?" he asks. As if we're in prison.

"Suicidal ideation."

"Really? Me, too. But you don't seem depressed."

"I'm not."

"I don't get it."

"Take a number."

He laughs. "What does your doctor say?"

"He doesn't say much. He listens. Sometimes he scolds me."

"For what?"

"Deflection. He doesn't like it when I want to talk about him. Does that make sense? We bare our souls and they get to remain strangers?"

He thinks for a long time.

"So you just kind of want to kill yourself?" he asks.

"No, I don't want to kill myself. That's why I'm here. I'm just pulled to do it."

"Why?"

I can't tell him.

Maybe I can tell him a little.

"I feel like there's something better."

He digests this, flicking his cigarette compulsively.

"Where?" he asks.

"Somewhere else."

"Like Heaven?"

"No. Not the Heaven you're thinking of."

"Like people sitting on clouds."

"Not like that."

He finishes his cigarette and steps on it and stares at it like he misses it.

"I don't want to go anywhere else," he says. "I just like the idea of it being over."

I don't tell him that it's never over. That would destroy his dream.

"Why don't you do it?" I ask.

"Because of my wife, Emily. I don't want to do that to her."

"That's a good reason."

"Otherwise I would have thrown myself off a bridge a long time ago."

"Have you always felt that way?"

"A long time. They say I'm Bipolar Type II. I'm on Lithium."

"Wow, that's powerful. They make batteries out of that."

"It makes me feel sluggish."

"But does it make you feel like living?"

He shakes his head. "It just takes away my motivation."

"I thought that was what pot was for."

He laughs. Every time he laughs it seems to surprise him, like running into an old friend.

I give him another cigarette and he tells me his story.

"I broke my arm snowboarding and then I had to stop surfing which was the only thing that ever kept me sane. I didn't connect the dots but I was getting more and more depressed. And then one night I was standing outside Jumbo's Clown Room, having a cigarette in the parking lot and talking to some dancer, and all of a sudden I felt really strange in my head. I thought it was going to explode. I thought I was going to get into my truck and drive it into a wall. So I called my wife and told her to come get me and that night she took me straight to the hospital and they kept me there and after a few days they recommended ECT so we decided to do it and then I didn't feel safe to go home so they sent me here."

He stops abruptly. I wait but he seems to be finished.

"Why were you at Jumbo's Clown Room?" I ask.

"What?"

"It's a strip club."

"No, it's a burlesque. They don't get actually naked."

"Okay."

"I like it there. I was with friends. Boys' night out."

"Your wife is okay with it?"

"Yeah. I don't fuck them or anything."

"Why do you think it happened there?"

"What happened?"

"Sudden breakdown."

"I don't know."

Shouldn't you know? I want to say. Isn't it worth asking? But I can see that would be taking it too far and after all, I'm not his therapist.

So I ask, "What was the dancer's name?"

He thinks. "Charmaine. But that was her stripper name. Her real name was Scarlet."

"Seriously?"

He nods and we start laughing and can't stop. The addicts are staring at us. Two crazies off the rails.

"Amazing that you remember that," I say.

He nods. "I usually remember the funny stuff."

CHAPTER FOURTEEN

David's therapist is a Jesuit priest. This is more than a coincidence. He and Father Joe Pasquale grew up together. They both attended Loyola High School. David's parents had no real use for the church other than an occasional superstitious pull around certain holidays. But they believed in Catholic education. He was exposed to most of his religious experience there at school. Some of his friends were lukewarm believers, some were completely indifferent, and in the margins were the devout—for and against. David counted himself among the devout against, and had no qualms describing himself as an atheist, skipping right over any agnostic phase. (He had no respect for agnostics; being willing not to know was a condition he had never understood.) But there he was, being best friends with Joe Pasquale who had no qualms about telling his peer group that he was considering the priesthood.

Joe was impervious to their ridicule, and accusations of homosexuality were too ridiculous to entertain. He was the quarterback of the football team and, as one friend said, had seen more ass than a rental car seat. Joe had no conflict with the idea that he was not exactly walking the path of the pious. His confirmation name was Ignatius. This saint was his role model, a man who spent the first half of his life not, as it were, being a saint.

"But he didn't know," David found himself arguing. "He had no idea about

Christianity. He was converted. He had a religious experience and swore off his old life."

"Yes," Joe said. "He decided to use his sword for Jesus."

"You are not using your sword for Jesus."

"I'm getting it out of my system. And anyway, I haven't made up my mind. What if I don't have a vocation? I will have wasted all that opportunity."

All of this was discussed while sneaking beer and cigarettes in the parking lot after class when Joe was supposed to be training and David was supposed to be working on the school paper.

So Joe had become a Jesuit priest and had also gotten a PhD in psychology and had gone on to be an analyst and counselor. When he was considering therapy for himself, David found Joe's name in the phone book. He felt it was fate even though he didn't believe in fate. And he suspected that Joe was the only person inside his profession with whom he'd ever consider making himself completely vulnerable.

They don't meet regularly. It is on an as-needed basis. And they don't socialize outside of these meetings. It is too confusing. In this, Joe is in agreement, and anyway, he works around-the-clock between his practice and his duties to the church.

Joe always wears street clothes for their sessions. Today he greets David in full top-to-bottom Calvin Klein casuals. He has a taste for good clothes and fine food. It all seems to conflict with his vow of poverty but, as usual, Joe does not seem disturbed by any such contradiction.

They exchange small talk and catch up on minor life events and politics. David is looking for a way to ease in but Joe, being good at his job, reads his expression and says, "What's on your mind, Dave?"

David smiles and stares at his feet. But when he looks up he's not smiling anymore. "Angels."

"Angels brought you here?"

"No. Questions about angels brought me here."

"Shoot."

"How do they work?"

"In what way?"

"Well, first, what are they?"

"They are inhuman spirits endowed with the responsibility to serve man."

"So they aren't like dead people who come back to help."

"People do not become angels when they die. Angels were never human. We are talking Catholic theology here. And for you, mythology. Metaphor."

"So that brings me to the tough question. Are they real?"

Joe laughs. "Do you think they're real?"

"Of course not."

"Then they're not real for you. Why are you suddenly curious?"

"I have a patient who is hearing from them."

"Really?"

"Well, she doesn't call them that. She calls them guides."

Joe nods, pressing his fingers to his lips. "I see," he finally says.

"Of course, where I'm coming from it's a delusion."

"It certainly could be," Joe says.

Silence blooms. David doesn't know where to look. He shifts in his seat. He can feel Joe waiting and he is envious of his patience. He remembers confession—not with Joe but in a dark booth with priests whose faces he couldn't see, even though he always knew who they were, given that there were only two priests in his parish. One smelled like spearmint and one smelled like nothing in particular. Spearmint priest always gave the easiest absolutions. Father Dennis. He was kind and quiet and seemed to think everything was going to be fine in the end. Father Smells-Like-Nothing (Monsignor Terrence) was harsher and talked more about Hell. David always chose to believe Father Dennis but who wouldn't?

He can't remember why he ever went to confession. It was some kind of morbid curiosity. It wasn't required of him by his parents or of his teachers. He has a vague sense of wanting to go there to see if he could shock the priests and because he never did, he eventually lost interest. But even as he's thinking about it, he misses it. Maybe it's why he went into this profession. He liked the idea of being the confessor. The anonymous yet familiar face on the other side of the screen. The desire to prove that he, like the priests, could not be shocked.

"What are you asking me exactly?" Joe says.

"I don't know. What do you think about these guides?"

Joe shrugs. "Could be anything. Could be brain chemistry. Could be delusions as you suggest."

"But could it be something else?"

"Sure."

"Joe. You're going to make me ask?"

"Yes."

David takes a breath and says, "Do you think these could be angels?"

Joe actually laughs.

"You're asking me hypothetical questions about a person I've never met."

"No, I'm asking what the church thinks about things like this. Visions and apparitions and modern-day saints. Does it happen? Is it frowned upon? What?"

Joe laughs. "I used to work with a Monsignor who said, 'The church hates miracles. All that paperwork.'"

"Be straight with me. Are angels real to you?"

"Why would it matter if they were real to me?"

"Because I trust you. I know you're smart and we're in the same profession."

"That wouldn't stop me from being crazy."

"Joe, help me out here."

"I can't, Dave. I can't give you faith. In either professional capacity. It's not transferrable. You have no idea how much I wish it were. It's my own struggle."

"Okay, then let's take it out of the personal. Tell me where the church stands on this."

Joe says irritably, "If you want to know what the church thinks, try going to church."

David just stares at his friend. He's relieved to see something of the bad Loyola boy remains, if only in the form of a mild temper.

Joe takes a breath and asks, "Does your patient present as stable otherwise?"

"Yes. Other than suicidal ideation, which is secondary to her communication with the guides. They give her feelings of bliss and she is, to use her word, homesick."

Joe nods. But there is more than comprehension in the nod. There is familiarity.

"Dave, is this part of a personal struggle?"

"I don't know."

"Are you infatuated with her?"

"Probably."

"And it's clouding your judgment."

"I hope not."

"But you're concerned."

"I'm concerned."

Joe stares at him for a moment, obviously gathering his words more than his thoughts. "Have you ever had this problem with a patient before?"

"Not since medical school. Maybe a couple years after. And even then, it wasn't like this. That was just sexual attraction. A little bit of the god complex."

"And this is not that?"

"No. I don't think about her sexually. I'm just drawn to her. There's something going on with her. I can't explain it."

"You're doing pretty well."

"It's not even so much how I feel around her. It's how I feel about the rest of my life when I'm away from her."

"And how is that?"

David thinks.

"My life feels shabby," he says.

Joe nods and presses his fingertips together. "Is this a new feeling for you?"

"Yes. I mean, like anyone, I question my choices. I wonder if I could be happier. But you get busy and the questions go away."

"And now they won't go away."

"Something like that."

Joe leans back in his chair and swivels it slightly so that he's staring out the window, and David isn't sure what to do.

"This is a dilemma," Joe finally says.

"I know."

"You're crossing into a place where I'm not sure how to help you."

David feels alarmed. He's never imagined himself beyond the help of a psychologist, let alone a priest.

"What place?" he asks.

"David, I'll just put it out there. You are having a spiritual crisis."

"How can I when I don't believe I have a spirit?"

"Belief is overrated," Joe says. "Belief is an intellectual construct. Who cares? Believing is an exhausting enterprise. Experience is everything. Belief is what you have in the absence of experience."

"Belief doesn't matter?"

"Well, it's a notch up from opinion."

"What are you talking about?"

Joe leans over his desk. "Jung said, 'I don't believe in God. I have come to know him.'"

David knows that quote. He says, "Good for Jung."

"He also said, 'Religion is a defense against a religious experience.'"

"I know what Jung said. But you're a man of belief!"

"I am not a man of belief. I am a man of faith."

David realizes there is an important difference but he's too tired to care. He slumps in his seat. Joe moves toward the slump.

Joe says, "Belief is about collecting ideas and investing in them. Faith is about having your ideas obliterated and having nothing to hang onto and trusting that it's going to be all right anyway."

David feels like crying. He sees his whole life's work circling the drain in the presence of what Joe is saying. He wants to respond but he doesn't know how.

Finally he blurts out, "I don't know what is happening to me."

"Sometimes God just comes after you," Joe says.

David locates a crumb of courage hiding in a place he forgot to look. He says, "Fuck God, he's too late."

But Joe only shrugs and says, "God is famous for looking like he's too late."

David sits for a moment, catching his breath, as if he has just run a marathon. He can feel, without seeing, the calm in Joe's eyes and it makes him wretched with envy.

"Okay, tell me about charisms."

"You know what they are," Joe says. "There are too many to list. There are those that Paul identified and there are many more that have been added by the church. You can have a charism for almost anything."

David hears Sarah's voice saying the word and then he's hurtled back through time, sitting in a desk in the eighth grade at Loyola while some priest is explaining charisms. He can see the list on the board. He knows the charisms were spelled out by St. Paul, though he can't remember which book of the Bible and he can't remember any of the charisms except the gift of speaking in tongues, which is probably when he checked out.

"Are they real?"

"You know they are. Call them talents if it makes you feel better."

"But they're more than talents."

"Yes. They are gifts of the Holy Spirit for the good of the community. They pull you against reason sometimes."

"So, compulsions."

"Sure, why not."

"Does everyone have them?"

"Yes, though not everyone pays attention to them or develops them. If it's a high-voltage charism and the person isn't spiritually prepared for one reason or another, then avoidance can ensue. And that can take many forms including addiction."

"It is too much to ask the average person to understand the difference between a compulsion and a calling."

"I agree."

"So how do we help them?"

"Gee, let's think. We could create a church and some sacraments."

"Work with me. So if a person is hearing voices, having visions and visitations…"

Joe cuts him off. "Discernment of spirits," he says.

"What?"

"That's what the charism is called. The one you're describing."

"They see dead people?"

"They have access in one form or another to the world of spirits. The world behind your eyes. Whatever is there. I don't have that charism so I can't speak from experience."

"Have you ever met anyone who did?"

"No. It's not the world I move in. I'm a Jesuit. I barely believe in God."

David laughs. He appreciates the levity. It pulls him back from the rabbit hole.

"I don't know what to tell you, Dave. God is out of the box."

"Why don't I feel better when I come here?" David asks.

"Every act of creation is first an act of destruction."

"If you quote Jung to me one more time I'm going to punch you in the face."

"I think that was Kierkegaard but welcome back."

CHAPTER FIFTEEN

Most of the saints talked about ecstasy. I only know this because I did some research once I started to think that these voices were not my imagination. I wanted to see how it was possible. I read about Teresa of Avila and John of the Cross and Joan of Arc and I still couldn't see how it was possible, but I was comforted by how familiar it all sounded. So that even if I was crazy, I was in good company.

Emanuel Swedenborg, for example, a Swedish philosopher and scientist from the eighteenth century, believed he had been granted the right to visit Heaven and Hell and report back on the conditions. He wrote a tome describing those dimensions and I read the tome and was impressed by how scientific it was, how unemotional, how specific, how conceivable. But it had to be crazy, right? He had to be crazy. Except that none of his colleagues thought of him that way. They continued to take him seriously as a scholar. None of his friends or colleagues ever reported on him seeming strange or having a breakdown while it was happening. He continued to serve in Swedish parliament and in the Royal Academy of Sciences. Later, of course, everyone except a few writers who were into the mystic declared him several sandwiches short of a picnic. But he continued to live a normal life, offending no one, and not particularly undone by his visions.

Imagine his conversations hanging out in the hallway outside Parliament.

"How's it going, Emanuel?"

"Can't complain. Just got back from Hell yesterday. Now, they have something to complain about."

Maybe that can happen to me. That's the best I can hope for. That this will settle down into something I can live with. That the voices will be more consistent. That I won't have to spiral into despair when they go away.

My friends will say, "How's it going, Sarah? Heard from Heaven lately? Any tips on the stock market?"

"No," I will say, in all seriousness. "If you abuse the charisms, you lose them. And the guides don't know everything, anyway. Only God knows everything."

"Interesting."

This is what Dr. Sutton is going to help me with. I don't know how. Neither does he. But we are giving it our best shot.

There's a subtle difference to him when he comes in. I am waiting in his office. After our last mix-up I want to be a little more obedient. And when the voices are talking, I am not as mischievous. I want to make things go smoothly. I don't want to upset Dr. David Sutton. But I do anyway because he comes in flustered.

"Ms. Lange, perhaps we should start off by discussing the nature of agreements."

"All right."

"The agreement we made, based on your needs, was to meet in the common room."

"I thought you preferred me to be here."

"I prefer there to be one consistent plan."

"Well, that's tricky with crazy people."

He ignores that. He is intense, on edge, but also a little intimidated by me in a way that I haven't seen before.

I want to take that tension away from him.

"Tell me what to do and I'll do it," I say. "Consistently."

"Then let's meet in this office at the appointed time."

"All right."

"I won't come looking for you. If you fail to show up here then we miss our appointment."

"Understood."

He sits and opens his briefcase and gets out his writing pad without looking at me. He takes several breaths through his nose then looks at me.

"Are you all right?" I ask him.

"Fine. How are you feeling today?"

"I feel great."

"I see. Is there a reason for that?"

"Yes."

"Do you want to discuss it?"

I think.

No, you don't.

"No, apparently I don't."

"Are you experiencing bliss?"

"So it doesn't matter that I don't want to discuss it."

He is momentarily stumped by that.

"What would you like to discuss?" he asks, inhaling patience.

"Anything else."

"All right."

He looks at his notes.

"Is it all right to talk about your near-death experience?"

I think. I listen.

"Yes, it is."

"Tell me about it."

"What about it?"

"Anything. What did you experience?"

I am able to talk about the attack now without thinking about it, without remembering it. I taught myself how to do that during the trial. But I've never minded talking about what happened when I died.

"He was choking me," I say. "That's how I died. He crushed my trachea. Later a doctor looked in my throat and said he had no idea why I was still alive. But then everyone was stumped by that."

"Go ahead."

"Okay, it was kind of a low-rent NDE. Not the fancy kind. No tunnels, no angels, no dead relatives. Not even a light. Suddenly I was just looking down on what was happening. Me lying on the bed and him choking me and I remember thinking, 'That looks like it would hurt.' Then I realized that I was out of my body. I could see everything around me. And here's what's strange. I felt more like myself than when I was in my body. It's you but it's you more intensely. It's pure consciousness. No ego, no contradictions, just pure self. It's hard to explain. Also, you're out of linear time. That's also hard to explain. And I realized I was surrounded by an intelligence. That's the only way I can describe it. I couldn't see it. I could only hear it but that's because its thoughts became my thoughts, and the feeling around it was very pleasant, and the tone of it was very neutral. It asked me two questions. The first one was, 'How much did you love and how much were you loved?' I was surprised to find that I hadn't loved very much and I hadn't been loved very much. And then I was asked if there was anything I'd like to go back for. And I must have said yes because I crash landed in my body and everything suddenly hurt."

"You don't remember saying yes."

"No."

"So you don't remember what you wanted to come back for."

"I thought we covered that."

"You always speak of these guides in the plural. Do they travel in twos?"

"Maybe. Or maybe it's that they don't have a word for I. It's not like that there."

He writes. He looks up.

"Might it be helpful to talk again about what you came back for?" he asks.

"That's surprising."

"Why?"

"It sounds dangerously as if you believe me."

"It doesn't matter if I believe your story in a literal way," he says. "I believe something happened to you and whatever it is, we can work with it symbolically. The fact that you gloss over the reason you came back is interesting to me. I think we should take a pick ax to that."

"What?"

"It's what Jung said. Take a pick ax to the thing you don't want to look at."

This time I'm the one who squirms. I try to disguise it as moving forward in my seat out of interest.

"If you don't know what you came back for," he says, "you might be confused about your purpose. It's not good to be confused about your purpose."

"So to make up for the fact that I have no purpose I'm creating imaginary friends?"

"I don't know," he says.

I press my hands against my temples.

"Are you all right?" he asks.

"Yes."

"Are you hearing something?"

"No."

He waits and I just stare at him.

He clears his throat to indicate a change of direction.

"After your near-death experience, this is when you started hearing from the guides on a regular basis?"

"I told you. I think I've heard them all my life. I just ignored them, pushed them down. You can do that. Most people do that."

"But then you stopped pushing them down. You started to acknowledge them. When was that?"

For some reason, this part is hard. It feels like he's getting too close to something, like he's trespassing inside my secret fort, even though I want him to visit the fort. Now he's in here and I don't know what to do with him.

"For about a year after the attack I had all kinds of voices and visions. Memories and flashbacks and self-recrimination and bargaining and things I should have said and done. It was a cacophony in my head. It was the sound of going crazy. I knew that. It was like a thousand radio stations playing at once. One day I couldn't take it anymore. It was just an ordinary morning in my kitchen, waiting for the kettle to boil. I dropped to my knees and begged, out loud, for it all to stop. And it almost did. The only thing left was this soft, neutral presence. Not a sound, not voices. Just a presence. And I demanded, out loud, to be told what that was. That's when they started talking. From that point on, if I asked, they answered."

I wait. He doesn't write. He just stares with those sea green eyes.

Finally he speaks: "So most people have guides. They just can't hear them."

I look at him as if he's just grown an extra head. "That's what you took from all that? I just told you the whole thing."

"I'm trying to clarify."

"I don't know about other people. I don't care about them most of the time."

He is frowning. He doesn't mean to and it's very subtle but he is disapproving. He hates the idea of God. People who hate the idea of God can't disguise it. But I don't care. Pleasing Dr. Sutton is not my job and saving him is not my business.

But he is drifting and it worries me because he is the one who is supposed to throw me a line back to earth. He's the one who is going to make the case for my staying here and playing well with others. How can he do that if he's on the fence himself?

"I'm trying to get to the root of your problem," he says.

"I will gladly tell you the root of my problem. The world is not enough."

He looks confused. "The James Bond movie?"

"It's a James Bond movie? No, I think I'm referring to something older. Alexander the Great, I seem to recall. It was on his gravestone. 'A tomb now suffices him for whom the world was not enough.'"

David nods and thinks. "Meaning you need more than what's in front of you."

"It's not about needing it. It's about belonging to it."

"If you belong to the other side, why are you here?" he asks.

But it's not a challenge. It sounds like a genuine question. It feels as if the power has shifted. The student has become the teacher.

"I don't know. I don't know."

He looks at me and I can hear the question he wants to ask: "Don't they tell you?"

I listen. They don't tell me.

I listen harder. I ask. Why am I here?

You know.

I don't know.

You know.

"I don't know!" I shout, and though the volume alarms Dr. Sutton, he thinks I'm still talking to him.

"All right. Take a breath. You don't have to know right now."

"It's like there are these two forces inside me. Inside everyone. One represents the real thing, the other is always trying to mislead us. No, that's not it. One is connected to the Divine and the other is trying to connect to the world. Trying to force the world into a safe place. Trying to get it to deliver in a way that it really can't."

Dr. Sutton says, "The ego cannot live in the absolute presence of God because it has to admit that it's not running the show and that's the ego's only function."

I look at him, surprised. "The ego?"

"Freud called it ego. Jung called it self. There are a number of ways to describe what you're talking about. I don't want to get too clinical."

"It's like we have to be in the world, not of it. Or what is that other thing about the garment?"

"St. Francis. Wear the world like a loose garment."

"That's it."

He stares at me, his face still, his mind tumbling. Dr. David Sutton is in the grips of something.

"Do you have a religious education?" he asks.

"Just dragged to some Protestant church till I was old enough to rebel."

He nods. After a moment he begins to write.

"But that's not where this is coming from, Dr. Sutton."

He keeps writing and finally puts his pen down and crosses his legs, looking at me in a way that creates dread in my stomach.

"Can we talk about medication?" he asks.

"No."

"I understand you're opposed to being sedated in any way and that you've refused to discuss antidepressants. We could put you on the mildest dose."

"Absolutely not."

"I really believe they would help."

"With what? I'm not depressed."

"I'm worried about your disorganized thinking."

"My thinking is disorganized?"

"Ms. Lange, you have a positive identification with suicide. That's a disorganized thought."

"In your world."

"It's the only world I can represent."

I smile.

"You believe you have no soul. That's a disorganized thought in my world."

Dr. Sutton closes his notebook and opens his briefcase.

We are done for the day.

CHAPTER SIXTEEN

Jen is already in the house when David arrives home. This fact irritates him. He might even say that it triggers him. Triggers a rage that boils up from some basement of which he is dangerously, or at least irresponsibly, unaware. He dislikes the use of the word "trigger" in his profession, though it is all but ubiquitous. He dislikes the idea of some nether psyche that is awakened by a sound or smell and has the power to take over. Why would there be a trigger or a fuse or a button or a hotspot in an otherwise functioning human being? As if the human psyche were riddled with trapdoors and land mines. He doesn't like to think about what that says about human nature. He doesn't like the idea of denying animalistic impulses. He prefers the idea of overcoming them, evolving out of them. He doesn't want to know about some sleeping giant in the heart or gut of a reasonable human. He doesn't like that idea in anyone and he especially doesn't like it in himself.

He reprimands himself for blaming his response to Jen on Jen herself. All she is doing is cooking in his kitchen. His reasonable brain should tell him that's a good thing, a generous thing, but he has to stand on the porch for a minute, breathing, so he won't accost her on sight. When he feels he has reined in his emotions, he opens the door and walks quietly into the kitchen. She is wildly chopping vegetables and throwing them into a wok in between taking swigs of wine. He stands for a moment watching her. He is trying to see her as a stranger. He is trying not to attach meaning to her presence. A lovely, skinny, tense woman with a tight ponytail in business attire throwing vegetables around his kitchen. Not worthy of anyone's wrath. Yet the wrath bites and licks at him. He breathes.

Seeing him, suddenly, she screams. The scream makes him jump and he drops his briefcase.

"Why do you do that?" she demands. "Why do you sneak around on little cat paws?"

"I don't mean to."

"You scared me. Jesus."

"I didn't expect to see you here."

"Why not?"

"I don't know. You don't show up unannounced that often. And you never start cooking without me."

"I couldn't wait," she says, hatcheting some broccoli.

He watches her and waits. He breathes into his rage, his triggers.

Eventually she slows down and turns to him, arms crossed.

"If you are interested," she says, "I was attacked today."

"Attacked?"

"Yes. By a nutcase at Oceanside."

"I was there today. I didn't hear about it."

"It wasn't on your side," she says.

"What do you mean by attacked?"

"Jumped on. Manhandled."

"My God. Are you okay?"

"Yes, obviously."

"Are you hurt?"

"My back has been better. The wine is helping."

"Do you want something stronger?"

"I've had half this bottle. I shouldn't mix."

"No, you shouldn't. Do you want to go to the ER?"

"No, I'll be all right."

He moves to the counter and pours himself a scotch. He feels her watching him.

"Do you want to talk about it?" he asks.

"Please don't use the therapist voice," she says.

"I didn't mean to use the therapist voice."

She sighs and shakes her head and undoes her ponytail in a rapid, angry move. She flushes out her hair and runs her fingers through it. He waits.

"Okay," she says. "Okay, if you want to hear I will tell you."

He nods.

She takes a deep breath and a forward bend. She comes back up, turns off the vegetables and takes another breath.

"There's this guy from your side. He used to be on our side. He was admitted for sex addiction. Then in group he started talking about suicide, so that idiot Susan Peltman decided he was probably more suited for trauma. To be honest, we were all relieved. None of us liked him. He had this thing. This way of hijacking group discussions. And it wasn't about his sex addiction, it was about how he had been done wrong at his last job and no one understood him and he was never good enough for his father and blah blah blah."

He takes his first sip of scotch and is grateful. It is thick and peaty and reminds him of playing in the woods as a child. Not here in L.A. so much but at the summer camp in Bakersfield where his parents sent him every year. The nearness of the earth, the call of the elements, the tease of fending for oneself, the rumbling of a storm far off which reminded him that he was not in charge. All of that in a glass of copper-colored liquid. He sips again for the purposes of grounding.

"So this guy went to the trauma side for a while, then decided he didn't like it there and came back to group today. He was all ready to admit to his disease. That's why they let him back in to group. They were so convinced they let him into my group, which, as you know, is for the highest functioning addicts. Those who have admitted to their disease and want to move on to the next step."

"Getting their lives in order."

"Exactly."

"So if this guy talked his way back in, he must be very convincing."

"Oh, he is convincing. He's also handsome. I swear, that's why Susan Peltman capitulated. She would let a serial killer into group if he had bedroom eyes and a square jaw."

"All right."

She sighs and deflates a little. "I know it's not rocket science. Attractive people always move mountains."

"So he's attractive."

"He's tall and has a full head of hair. It's almost white, even though he's in his early forties. His name is Kit. Though that's not entirely the truth. His name on his admittance form is Christopher Kelly."

"Kit sounds like a reasonable nickname."

"You know how I distrust nicknames. It's a form of hiding."

He stares at her for a moment. The scotch has unleashed his tongue.

"You go by Jen," he says.

"I do not! I go by Jennifer at work. Dr. McCrady if anyone cares but they usually don't. They are so fond of first names at this place."

"I have a rule about that."

"Yes. I know. I am starting to understand your rule. I used to think it was anal but now I see the point."

She takes a breath and another sip of wine, putting her glass down with a loud clink.

"So we're in session and this guy, Kit, is trying to take over the discussion. I'm talking about authentic actions and such. You know that's what I'm in the business of. Authentic actions rather than complaining."

"Yes."

"And most of the group are hearing me, following me. But he keeps resisting. He says, 'What the hell is an authentic action? What if I wanted a drink? Or meaningless sex? Wouldn't that be an authentic action?' I said authentic actions are different from defensive actions, all that stuff, and soon the group starts to speak against him. 'No,' he says, 'no, I don't want to hear rhymes and theories. We are talking about authenticity. I authentically want to go out and get hammered and fuck someone I don't know.' Now a small subsection of the group begins to applaud."

David feels the danger building in her story. He wants to be in the room to stop what's happening.

"Susan Peltman tries to weigh in, saying, 'Let's redirect our focus,' or whatever nonsense she says. But the next thing you know, the whole group is baying for blood. They want the authentic action of taking a drink. Susan stands and starts yelling at them, calling them bargain-basement drunks, which I guess is emergency language for addicts. They ignore her. Suddenly it's like a scene from *One Flew Over the Cuckoo's Nest* and she is Nurse Ratchet."

Jen sees the smile tugging at the corners of his lips.

"Is this funny to you?"

"Not at all. It's just the way you are telling it. I thought you were trying to be funny."

She is diverted momentarily, as if imagining herself as a good storyteller. She shakes it off and continues.

"Now this guy Kit is on his feet and he is clapping and doing that cheer from…what is it, *Meatballs*? The one with Bill Murray?"

David nods, remembering. "It just doesn't matter."

"That's right. He's clapping and saying, 'It just doesn't matter. It just doesn't matter.' Now everyone in the group is clapping and chanting, 'It just doesn't matter.'"

David is engaged now. He feels as if he's watching a movie.

"Then what?"

"Then what do you think? The whole group is on their feet. They are walking in a circle, chanting, 'It just doesn't matter.' Susan finds her walkie-talkie and asks for security. They don't answer. I can see this is going nowhere good. But I can also see that the leader has to be brought down. It's like some tin dictator. If I can get rid of him, I can restore peace. So I stand and approach Kit and I say, 'Sit down or this will end badly.' You know what he says to me? Do you want to know what this guy says to me?"

"Of course."

"He says, 'Lady, it's all going to end badly. That's how it ends.'"

David feels the smile creeping up again.

"David," she says, "I'm appalled by you. You think this is funny."

"No. I don't. But I think it's accurate."

"Accuracy is not the point."

"I'm sorry. Go ahead."

Jen takes a long sip of wine and then holds the glass tightly in her hand. She stands very straight and looks him in the eye.

"This guy Kit grabs me. Grabs me by the arms. I try to wrestle away but he is too strong. He puts me in a choke hold. I feel like I am dying. My life flashes before my eyes. Susan is screaming into the walkie-talkie and the others start to mumble and cry. But Kit keeps on pressing into my neck. I look in his eyes. I see he wants to kill me. I have never seen a thing like that before. I have never seen a thing, let alone a person, that wanted to kill me. But he did."

David puts his glass of scotch down. He reaches for her without touching her. He is afraid to touch her. He is aware that she is afraid of being touched.

"Jen, I'm so sorry. Are you okay?"

She sniffs and shakes her hair, and finally peels back the collar of her starched white blouse to reveal plum-colored bruises around her neck.

"Dear God," he says. "He did that?"

"He did that," she says, then bows her head and cries into her hand. "I didn't want to show you."

"Why not?"

"It's embarrassing."

"Why are you embarrassed? Can I touch you?"

She shakes her head, still covering her face. "It hurts too much."

He puts a hand on her arm anyway and asks again why she's embarrassed.

"Because I know you don't respect what I do," she says. "And it's like I'm getting what I deserve."

"Don't say that. How could you think that about me?"

"I don't. I think it about me."

"You're just in shock. Sit down, please."

She allows herself to be led to a chair. He hands her the glass of wine but she's still crying too hard to even hold it. He puts it on the table next to her. He waits for a cue from her.

"I'm just a life coach," she sobs. "I'm just trying to help them learn how to live."

"I know."

"I'm not like you. I'm not nice. But that doesn't mean I don't care. I don't give a fuck about what hurt them or derailed them. I just want them to get well. I want them to have a chance."

"I know. I know."

She sobs for a few more seconds and still he doesn't know what to do.

Finally she looks up. Her face is wet and ruined like a six-year-old's.

"I don't think I can go back there."

"You shouldn't for a while."

"I mean ever. And I mean my profession."

"You don't have to make that decision right now."

"But how am I going to get through my days?"

"Let's just worry about this one."

He sits down beside her and takes her hand.

"I guess you can try to hug me," she says.

He puts his arms around her. She leans in to him.

A sliver of a poem he remembers from freshman English floats up out of nowhere:

Where can we live but days?
Ah, solving that question
Brings the priest and the doctor
In their long coats
Running over the fields.

CHAPTER SEVENTEEN

The day after Kit tries to kill the doctor, Willie's wife Emily comes to visit him. I stand at a window in the common room, watching them out in the garden. They're sitting on a bench next to a fountain and she is talking fast and touching his knee and his arm and his hair, grooming him like a simian mate, and he is staring at the ground and flicking his cigarette. Sometimes he nods. Emily is a short perky woman with surfer-girl hair and a button nose and perfect posture. I like her energy. I can almost see her aura. I don't see auras and I've never wanted to learn because I don't need even one more superpower and because I secretly believe people are lying when they say they see auras the way they think I am lying when I say I hear from guides. We don't believe in what we can't experience. And we are always jealous of other people's powers. That's one of my many theories. I can't share them because no one ever asks. Maybe Dr. Sutton will ask one day but I think he's more interested in his own theories, which leak out from time to time even when I don't ask.

I have the common room completely to myself except for the attendants. The regular crazies wanted to be in their rooms today and the suicidals all asked to see their doctors. I didn't. That has made the attendants circle around me with watchful eyes. I never mind seeing Dr. Sutton but I also never feel compelled to see him. The head of Oceanside, a Hillary Clinton type in a structured suit of unfortunate color, called an emergency meeting to explain to us what happened with Kit and to tell us that we should all take special care of ourselves in this difficult time. Some of us might get triggered, she said. Some of us might be retraumatized just by hearing the story, she said. That is how PTSD works, she said. Some of the crazies wanted details. Did the guards really shoot Kit? Real bullets or rubber or a tranquilizer dart? Is the doctor really paralyzed now? Was it the life coach lady or Dr. Peltman? Was there a riot? Was it really some Bill Murray cult thing?

Hillary Clinton (her name is actually Dr. Frankenheimer and everyone calls her Frankenstein or just Frank) pushes the manic energy back down with the palms of her hands and says, "It was Dr. McCrady, who has a number of degrees including a PhD, so let's not call her 'the life coach lady.' She is recovering from minor injuries. Mr. Kelly was not shot with anything. He was subdued by the guards and later given a sedative in the clinic. He has been transferred to another location and you need not worry about him. There was no riot and no cult of any kind. It was just a group session that got out of hand because as we now know, Mr. Kelly's condition was far too advanced for us. He needs stronger supervision and serious medical attention. We're sorry this had to happen but at least Mr. Kelly can move on to make progress and order is restored here at Oceanside. It is still your safe place. But we encourage you to take the steps you need tomorrow and the rest of the week to reassure yourselves of that. We will be offering any of the individual services you request."

She went on to say that the common-room hours would be extended and a special meal was being donated by Spago and I can't even remember what else because it all sounded like bribery. The subtext was "don't sue." As if any of us were motivated enough to find a litigator and as if any judge would take something we had to say seriously. Then I remembered that most of the crazies had families and families do like to sue on behalf of their problem children. It's better when there is someone to blame. It's better when the problem child can be some sort of cause célèbre. "I did this so that no one else ever has to feel this kind of pain again." That's what people say when they exploit their misfortune.

I remember looking at Willie during this meeting and he smiled at me and shook his head as if he found the whole ordeal ridiculous. Later, sitting together over the Spago meal, he leaned into me and said, "Go, Kit. Too bad he didn't kill her."

"Did you know her?"

"She's a cunt."

"So you know her."

"I've seen her."

"How do you know she's a cunt?"

"You can tell. Just the way she walks."

I smile. "I don't think they zapped all that rage out, Will."

"Nah, they left a little just for me."

"That was nice of them."

"I think of taking that lady, what's her name? With the stiff hair and the flapping hands?"

"Dr. Frankensomething."

"I think of taking her and putting her head through a wall."

"It might only hurt the wall."

He laughs hard, then abruptly stops as if he's forgotten the conversation.

"You're completely nuts, you know that," I say.

"Oh, yes."

"I like that in a person."

Now I am watching the gentle giant, who might not be so gentle after all, sitting like a great blond Wookie, listening to his wife talk about—what, I wonder? Her work? I can't remember what he says she does. I can't remember if he ever said. She looks like an accountant. Like the bookkeeper for some company full of men and she loves keeping them in line and making fun of them and they like telling her their problems and making her laugh. Is she telling him stories from her work? Is he trying to listen or just pretending to listen?

I have thoughts about Willie that disturb me. I have pictures. I picture us kissing behind the ceramics shed. I picture us stealing a car and running away. Robbing banks across the country. Living in Mexico in a clay hut. Crazy outlaw pictures. I have no idea where they are coming from. They don't feel like visions. They feel like temptations. When the pictures come I don't hear the voices and I don't miss the voices. These pictures are the only things that make me not miss the voices. I hope Willie will leave soon. I hope he will never leave. Paradoxes dance in my head.

"Ms. Lange?"

The voice makes me jump. It is not a stern voice but it is loud. Feels loud, breaking into my paradoxes that way.

It is Dr. Sutton standing in the common room. For a second I feel as if I am seeing him through a fish-eye lens. His face is wide and his nose protrudes and his glasses have a life of their own and he's wearing a nerdy professor suit from the fifties. Then the distortion eases and it's only Dr. Sutton with normal features and normal glasses but the same nerdy professor suit from the fifties.

"We don't have an appointment," I say.

"I know."

"That's why I'm in the common room. Because we don't have an appointment."

"I'm aware."

"So I can't be in trouble."

"You are not in trouble."

"Then why are you here?"

"Because of the incident."

I have momentarily forgotten, caught up in my outlaw dream.

"Oh, the thing with Kit?" I ask.

"The incident with Dr. McCrady."

"The life coach lady."

"Dr. McCrady."

"Is she okay? They said she's okay. Minor injuries."

"She will be fine."

She has curly hair but she straightens it.

"What?" he asks.

Apparently I have said this out loud.

I am backed in now so I repeat it.

"I don't see how that's relevant," he says.

"She's your girlfriend."

"I believe we've been over this."

"No. You accused me of asking around but I didn't so I didn't really know if my information was accurate. I mean, it usually is, but I didn't put it all together until just now."

"Dr. McCrady is my girlfriend."

I see he hates the word girlfriend but he hates the alternatives more. Partner. Significant Other. Lover. Special Friend. Colleague. Fellow Outlaw.

"I'm very sorry," I say. "About what happened. Not that she's your girlfriend."

"I am as well. But she is strong. She will come back."

"She's not checking in here, is she?"

"What? Of course not."

"Because she's been traumatized."

"Yes, but..."

"But she doesn't get PTSD because she's strong? Unlike the rest of us here."

"I did not mean that at all."

"But it's what you said. You said she's strong. Of course she's not checking in here."

He clears his throat. "This is why I do not like to stray from the deliberate path of our work."

"But it happened here. So we have to talk about it. Your girlfriend is stronger than the rest of us. Let's talk about that, Dr. Sutton."

"Let's go to my office."

"In a minute. Just solve this riddle for me."

He takes a deep breath and his face goes pink. "It is not that she's stronger than the rest of you. It's that she has never been traumatized before. And because she has the tools to cope with it, because she knows what those tools are, she can process it in an appropriate way."

"I see."

"Most of the people here, including yourself, were traumatized in childhood and retraumatized throughout your life and you had no appropriate coping skills. What we do here is try to teach you, to give you..."

"Tools?"

"Tools, yes. For coping."

"What's your favorite tool?"

"We are not going to talk about me today, Ms. Lange."

"But we kinda are."

"Not anymore. Would you like to retire to my office?"

"I'm not even sure I want this session. What is it, a special charity session? Because I might be triggered?"

The use of the word trigger changes his expression.

"Why do you say that?" he asks.

"Because that's what they keep telling us here. We might be triggered."

His face relaxes. "I see."

"But it makes me feel like a horse, you know?"

He laughs. His shoulders move away from his ears.

"Of course, you're not required to have this session."

"What the hell. You came all the way out here."

We retire, as he says, to his soulless office and I sit on the industrial gray couch and he sits in an industrial metal and black leather chair. He doesn't take out charts and writing materials. This means he's only checking on my immediate state of mind.

"How are you feeling?" he asks.

"Fine."

"No anxiety? No nightmares?"

"Nightmares?"

"Replaying the event in your mind?"

"I didn't witness it."

"But you can imagine it."

"I try not to imagine things."

"Why is that?"

"Because my reality is overwhelming as it is. I don't need to add."

"Can you control that?"

"Mostly."

Red clay hut in Mexico.

"You know, imagination is not a bad thing. It's in fact a vital component of creativity," he says.

"I try not to create either."

"But you're a writer. And an artist."

"Was."

He ignores the past tense. "And you employed your imagination then."

"I attempted to commit art and poetry when I was a kid. That is such a small fraction of my life. What I've done as an adult is something else. Employment. It doesn't involve the imagination."

"Not at all?"

"No. And neither does artistic expression, come to think of it."

"No?"

"I told you, that isn't how art works."

"Did you tell me?"

"I thought so."

"Tell me again."

I sigh. "The poem, the drawing, the painting…it already exists. You just pull it out of the ether. You transcribe it. A little something is always lost in the translation. That's why we get depressed."

"Because in your imagination it was perfect."

"No. No. Because where it lives it is perfect."

"Where does it live?"

"On the other side."

"You're saying that you channel these concepts?"

"They exist. If you are quiet you can experience them. If you are willing, you can render them. Then other people can experience them."

He frowns while thinking about this.

"You want to write something down?" I ask.

"No. I'm just processing."

"With your tools?"

A tight smile. He doesn't answer.

The processing goes on for another moment. I shift in my seat.

"Do you want a cigarette?" he asks.

"No. I just want to go back to where I was."

"Home?"

"No, the common room."

"So you don't want this session after all?"

"I don't want any more of it."

"Very well. Just reassure me that your thoughts have not become morose."

"My thoughts are rarely morose."

"Let me rephrase that. That you aren't feeling the pull. Any stronger. Than usual."

"Oh, no. In fact, I'm feeling it less."

"Good."

"Is it?"

"Yes, Ms. Lange. We want you here."

"At Oceanside?"

"In the world."

"Yes. There is much to do here. I am starting to see that."

"Good," he says. "I'm very glad to hear it."

He stands up, is very still for a moment, staring at the middle distance, and then he sits back down. This action of his makes me feel exhausted. I don't know how to get rid of him. He opens his briefcase and pulls out a tattered paperback book. I can't see the title.

He says, "I'd like to read you something I came across the other day. Are you familiar with Joseph Campbell?"

He flashes the front of the tattered book in front of me. It has a mandala on the cover but otherwise means nothing much to me.

"Not really," I say.

It's a lie. I know who Joseph Campbell is. Back when I was whoever I was before, I watched his interviews with Bill Moyers and read his collected works and was astounded by his insight as everyone with a college degree and a modicum of interest in mythology or literature was. The truth is, I loved Joseph Campbell back when I was—what? Participating in the real world? Back then it sounded like something I already knew. I was drawn to it. Now I want to hear what Dr. David Sutton has to say about him.

He says, "He is…was…a mythologist. Which is to say he was a person who devoted his life to translating mythology. He was more than that, though. He elevated those myths into an understanding of psychology. He was a student of Jung. He tilled a lot of ground in helping us forge the worlds of myth and psychology, using the tools of symbolism and archetypes."

I nod, listening, suppressing a yawn. I pity the poor student who ever hopes to learn about Joseph Campbell from Dr. Sutton. He is making it about as interesting as paint thinner.

He doesn't read my expression because he doesn't really seem to read expressions. Instead, he opens the book and flips to a dog-eared passage.

Before he reads he says, "This is something I came across and it made me think of you."

"Okay."

I hope to God it's not some kind of love or kindred spirit passage.

He starts to read, robotically:

"'The artist is the true seer and prophet of his century, the justifier of life and as such, of course, a revolutionary far more fundamental in his penetration of the social mask of his day than any fanatic idealist spilling blood over the pavement in the name simply of another unnatural mask.'"

He closes the book and looks at me.

"Do you have any thoughts about this?" he finally asks.

"Not really. Do you?"

He stares at the book as if it is guiding him.

"I was thinking of you as an artist," he says.

"But I'm not."

"But you were."

"Well." I shrug.

"Do you think that's something you can just abandon?"

"No. I think of it as something that can abandon me."

"You feel abandoned by your calling?"

My skin starts to itch. I scratch my neck. He watches me.

"What do you want to know?" I finally ask.

"I was thinking of why you came back. From your near-death experience."

I actually laugh out loud. The laugh seems to wound him. He recoils and begins to blush. I know he can feel the blood rushing to his face and I know he feels ashamed of this. But he stares straight at me. He has taught himself this stare. He believes this stare is some kind of shield that makes him invincible. Even though on some level he must know it exposes him altogether.

I say, "You think I came back from the dead to paint some landscapes?"

He doesn't respond. I realize that he has had a moment prior to this, the way a lover has a moment in the middle of the night when he realizes the exact thing he needs to say and is willing to run across flooded fields in the rain and shirtsleeves and bare feet to say the thing he forgot to say to the person in question and then it will all be okay. And now I am saying it is not all okay.

I am sorry for his disappointment but I cannot help him with it.

"I don't know," he says, sitting up straight, becoming the dry scientist in the fifties suit. "I just found it interesting and I thought you would, too."

"I don't find it uninteresting," I say. Which is the equivalent to saying I love you but I'm not in love with you.

Metaphorically, Dr. Sutton is standing before me in drenched clothes, his epiphany rejected and denounced by a callous would-be lover.

In reality he stands in dry clothes, collects his things and says, "I'm sorry for coming over. I didn't mean to intrude."

"You didn't intrude. It's good to see you."

"I'll be back for our regular appointment."

I watch him until he reaches the door and hits the buzzer and is released from his duty by a short guy dressed all in white, keys dangling.

———·———

I make my way back to the common room.

When I return to the window, Willie and Emily are no longer in the garden. I watch the spot where they were sitting for a long time until it begins to rain and then I can't see the picture anymore. Something else is taking its place. I am starting to see a different picture.

CHAPTER EIGHTEEN

David is in session with his favorite bulimic when the call comes.

His favorite bulimic is a fifteen-year-old boy named Sebastian. Bulimic and anorexic males are rare. The symptoms most often present in gay males and Sebastian is no exception. He is the only son of a wealthy real estate tycoon. His four sisters are all high achievers, athletes, and he, the youngest, has dragged his father's dreams of legacy into a quagmire. Sebastian is not so much concerned with how his father sees him as how the world sees him.

"Well, of course I'm trying to disappear," Sebastian says. "The world wants me to disappear. And I'm a rule follower."

"I don't think it's fair to say the world wants you to disappear," David says.

"Okay, then just my father and 90 percent of the country."

"As far is the country is concerned, I'm sure the statistics are skewed. And even if that were accurate, there are places in the world..."

"So Morocco likes me. And Athens. I live here, Dr. Sutton."

"Sebastian, we all have things about us that the world at large rejects. Artists, for example. The world rejects them."

"Yeah," Sebastian says. "I'm also an artist."

"All right, that's a bad example. Psychiatrists. Much of the medical world rejects us."

"Really?"

"Sure. We're considered a weak discipline. Witch doctors."

"I think you're reaching."

"I'm not. I experience feelings of rejection all the time. For example, it might surprise you to know that my own father does not approve of my profession."

"Well, he's just being a bitch. I mean, you're straight. You are, aren't you?"

"Yes."

"And you have a medical degree."

"Yes."

"So your father is just being a bitch."

"And what is your father being? Reasonable?"

Sebastian thinks about it, staring out the window. "He has a legitimate complaint."

"No, he doesn't."

"You don't know my sisters. They are assholes."

"I believe we are getting off point."

Sebastian examines his nails for a moment, then looks up. "You're married, right?"

"No," David says. "I am not married."

"But you have a girlfriend."

"I do."

"And you're probably going to marry her, right?"

David looks away. As usual, he is surprised that his therapy session has wandered off down the path of his personal life. As a therapist, he has to wonder if he allows such a thing to happen, if he somehow uses his sessions for his own purposes, to shed light on his own psyche. He hopes not but he cannot swear to it lately.

Is he going to marry Jen? He knows, now more than ever, that he is not. Her behavior following the attack has turned erratic and strange. She has nightmares. She has a heightened startle reflex. She has trouble swallowing. She doesn't want to leave her apartment. She misses work. She has developed an habitual coffee ritual and is experiencing panic attacks.

She asked him to prescribe her medication. He refused.

"Why not?" she railed. "Don't you know what I am going through?"

"You should see a doctor," he told her.

"But you're my doctor."

"I can't be."

"Why not?"

"Because. I cannot sleep with my patients."

"Then I don't see the problem," she said.

He swallowed the insult and powered on. "You need to see a doctor. I can't be your doctor. You of all people should know that."

But she waved a hand at him, pacing, crazy. "All this separation we insist upon. As if we're trying to keep the sane away from the crazy. No one is sane. We're all crazy. What is this nonsensical team sport, like we're all in the seventh grade wearing different colored pinnies? Red for sane, blue for crazy. We're all in the same soup. Why can't you help me?"

"Because I'm not qualified."

"You're a goddamned doctor. You're not qualified?"

"I'm not qualified as your partner."

"When have you ever been my partner?"

He forgives her hurtful outbursts. He knows she is still in shock. He did give her the names of several therapists but she didn't go. Her life-coaching beliefs have been hardened against that profession. Talk talk talk, she used to say. It was an endless cycle of self-pity and reinforcement of the ego, she once said.

"But cognitive behavioral therapy is not like talk therapy," he argued. "It's proactive. You'll have homework. Goal setting. More like what you do."

"I don't need homework, David, I need some drugs to calm down what's misfiring in my brain. It's a chemical issue. It's neurotransmitters."

So he gave her the names of some psychiatrists.

"No," she declared, actually tearing up the piece of paper. "I do not want to sit in some guy's office and talk about my parents for a half a dozen sessions before they decide what I really need is a drug."

"What is it, Jen? Is life about a lack of direction and goal setting, or is it about chemicals in the brain? You can't have it both ways. Are you a unique creation in the history of time, as I've heard you say, or are you a bag of chemicals, a machine that has thrown a piston?"

"Leave it to you to use my work against me," she said.

"I'm not doing that."

"Yes, you are."

"How can I use your work against you when I don't entirely understand it?"

"Exactly. You don't understand it."

"I'm admitting that!"

"I was hurt, David! As a human being. I was hurt and nearly killed."

"I know that. And I've tried to reach you on that level but..."

"I don't have a level. What the fuck are you talking about with levels? I'm not a goddamned elevator."

"I know that."

"You don't know that."

"All right. I don't know that. Tell me how to reach you."

"I shouldn't have to tell you!"

"That's not fair," David found himself saying.

And she stood with a straight back and said, "Aren't you the one who is always telling me life is not fair but it is just?"

David took a moment to contemplate that.

"No, I'm not the one who is always saying that. But it's pretty true."

"It's pretty true? How can something be pretty true? Either it's true or it's not."

"I don't know," David said, hoping to end the discussion.

"Either a thing is true or it's not," Jen insisted.

It was exhausting. All of this was exhausting. Maybe it was why he said what he said next.

"It's like the Heisenberg principle. Before that, everyone thought light was a wave. No, maybe a particle. Then when they saw it behave both ways they decided it could be both. Just so they could move on. So they didn't have to ask, 'Why is it both? How is it both?' They left it at both and no substantial work has been done in the area of electrodynamics since. Because they didn't want to break down the paradox. They didn't want to know that light might be intelligent. That it might make the choice of whether to behave as particle or wave. They didn't want to know."

"David..."

"Like when Newton discovered that all color came from white light. People didn't want to know. They jumped off buildings."

"David, fuck's sake, we're not talking about physics. We're talking about human emotion. Human involvement."

"You can't go around pain, Jen. You can only go through it," David said.

"Jesus. What's up with you? You're a psychiatrist. You're telling me there's no way around it? You don't give your clients drugs?"

"Patients. I give my patients drugs when I've exhausted all other possibilities."

"I've exhausted all other possibilities."

"You haven't even started."

"This is so easy for you to say. No one has ever tried to kill you."

He thought about that. He thought about the man who had dragged him out of his wrecked car and hit him. He remembered that man's face. That man wanted to kill him. But he hadn't taken it personally. He took it as a mental breakdown. No, less than that. Just an impulse to give in to the weaker side. Rage, and the target was moving.

"Dr. Sutton," Sebastian is saying. "Are you still with me?"

David looks at him, coming out of his trance. He has allowed himself to drift off, something he never does. Or thinks that he never does.

"Yes, Sebastian, I apologize."

"It's okay. Shrinks have problems, too, I guess."

And this is when his phone rings. It is his private cell phone, which he keeps on during sessions because it is only for emergencies. It never rings. Everyone in his life knows what a true emergency in his world amounts to.

"I'm sorry, I have to get this."

"No problem," Sebastian says and takes out his own phone to check his emails and messages.

David scrambles through his briefcase and finds the phone and looks at the number which is unfamiliar to him. He is tempted to ignore it. But he sees that Sebastian is smiling at something on his iPhone screen and decides to take the moment.

"This is Dr. Sutton."

"Dr. Sutton, this is Melinda Frankenheimer at Oceanside."

"I'm in session," he says.

"I understand. We have this listed as your emergency number."

"What's wrong?"

"It's your patient, Sarah Lange."

His heart catches. "Is she all right?"

"Well, we're not entirely sure. She has disappeared."

"Disappeared? Into thin air?"

"In the gardener's truck."

"Excuse me?"

"Sometime this morning. She stole his truck. He often leaves the keys in it. We've asked him to stop doing that. Anyway, she must have known. She must have been thinking about this for a while."

"But why? She's voluntary. She can leave anytime."

"Perhaps you should come out here. We can speak more freely. And the police want to have a word with you."

"The police?"

"It's grand larceny, Dr. Sutton. And kidnapping."

"Kidnapping?"

"She took another patient with her."

His palms are sweating and he feels the way he did in medical school, the one time he thought about cheating on a lab test. He hadn't done it but the fact that he thought about it felt like some tangible malfeasance.

"But why would they want to talk to me?" he asks.

"Because you're her doctor."

"But I don't know anything."

"Dr. Sutton, you're not a suspect. You're just a witness. Can you please come out here?"

Reason descends on him like a steel trap. He's in the grips of it. He's not sure why he ever abandoned it. He feels ashamed for his momentary lapse. "Yes, of course. I'll be right there."

He hangs up and finds Sebastian still staring at his iPhone, giggling.

"Sebastian, I am terribly sorry. There's an emergency. I have to cut our session short."

Sebastian looks up. "Uh-oh. Did one of your patients off themselves?"

"No. Nothing like that."

"I guess you get a lot of that, though."

"No. As a matter of fact, that very rarely happens."

"You don't have to worry about me, either. I'm just gonna go home and eat some blueberry Eggos and barf them."

"That's your prerogative."

"Here again, just kidding. You need to lighten up, Doc."

"Same time next week? Or if you'd like to schedule an additional hour."

"Don't worry about me. Go ahead. You're the color of tapioca. It's not attractive."

——•——

There are several police cars in front of Oceanside when he arrives. He shows his credentials and they wave him through. Inside, the common room is completely empty. A kind of lockdown has occurred, he surmises. All of the trauma patients sent to their rooms like children who shouldn't see their parents' fighting. A very young woman in an ill-fitting business suit approaches him. She has been pacing and looking at her phone. She seems to recognize him right away, though they've never met.

"Dr. Sutton? I'm Courtney Dreiser. I handle P.R. for Oceanside."

"P.R.?"

"Come this way."

He follows her down a long hallway to the administrative offices, where he hasn't been since his first interview. Courtney's heels clack on the tile floor. He feels a sweat breaking out on his forehead and he wipes it with his jacket sleeve. Courtney casts a sympathetic glance over her shoulder.

"Big times here at Oceanside," she says.

He says nothing to that. Her heels clack.

"What with the incident with Dr. McCrady. Now this."

He still says nothing.

"Dr. Frankenheimer is anxious to see you."

"All right," he says.

They arrive at Dr. Frankenheimer's door and she smiles at him and taps. A brief wait and then the door is opened by a man with sallow skin and a moustache, wearing a weathered jacket and polyester tie.

Courtney says, "Detective Jackson, Dr. Sutton."

"Oh, yeah, thanks, hon," Detective Jackson says.

Courtney takes the time to deliver an eye roll before clacking away.

Dr. Frankenheimer stands and comes around her desk and offers her hand, as if they are about to enter into a complicated business deal.

"Dr. Sutton. Thank you so much for coming. You've met Detective Jackson."

"Yes."

Jackson gives him what appears to be a smirk and collapses into a leather armchair and takes out a notebook. David remains standing until Dr. Frankenheimer gestures toward the chair opposite the detective. He doesn't want to sit but he knows he must sit. He does.

"Well, this is quite a predicament," Frankenheimer says, leaning against her desk. She is staring at the two of them as if they have somehow been involved in a high school prank. He can feel Jackson looking at him but does not return the look.

"You can imagine," Frankenheimer says, "how difficult this is for us. On top of what happened with Jen."

"Excuse me, who's Jen?" Jackson asks.

"Dr. McCrady," David says.

"Yes, Dr. McCrady. I've already explained, David, that you and she are intimately acquainted."

David clears his throat. "I don't see how that's relevant."

Jackson says. "In the past two weeks here at Oceanside, there have been incidents of abnormal behavior. And you bear some connection to both of those incidents."

"I'm sorry. What happened with Jen...Dr. McCrady...really had nothing to do with me. We don't even work on the same side."

"Side?" Jackson asks.

Frankenheimer says, "We isolate the groups here. Mr. Kelly and Dr. McCrady were on the addiction side. Dr. Sutton works exclusively on the trauma side."

"I see."

Jackson writes something down and there is an insufferable pause. Frankenheimer lifts her eyebrows in David's direction and he has no idea what all this eye language is supposed to mean. David clears his throat again.

"Perhaps if someone could tell me what happened," he says.

Jackson says, "What happened is that five days after your girlfriend was assaulted here, one of your patients stole the gardener's truck and took off with another patient here. William Cranston. Do you know him?"

"No. I am not on staff here. I am called in to consult. Ms. Lange is my only patient here at the moment."

"Except she's not here at the moment," Jackson says.

"I'm just finding this out, Detective. I need a moment to process it."

"Sure, I understand."

"Would you like some water?" Dr. Frankenheimer asks.

"No, thanks."

He sees that his hands are shaking and he interlaces his fingers hoping to control them. He feels the detective watching him. He tries not to take it personally. It's what detectives do. They detect.

Frankenheimer takes a deep breath. "David, we have no idea what's happening here. I've been at Oceanside for ten years and we've never had anything…anything…remotely like this occur. For the most part, this is a voluntary hospital. People don't have to run away."

"I'm aware."

"And we have almost no record of violence. Some patients when they first come in fight against detox. But we don't have patients suddenly attacking the therapists. That just doesn't happen."

"Are you accusing me of something?"

Jackson waves a hand and says, "You understand, I'm a cop, and I'm trained to follow evidence. And sometimes evidence looks like coincidence. We have a big coincidence here."

"Yes," David says.

"Now maybe it's just a coincidence, your connection to these two incidents, because coincidences happen."

"Yes, they do."

"But you see how I have to look into those kinds of things."

"Certainly. Of course."

"I'd like to talk to you about your patient, Sarah Lange."

"That's confidential information."

"We don't want you to open the books," Frankenheimer says. "Just lead us in some direction. Last time you saw her, which I believe was on the same day that Dr. McCrady had her incident?"

"The day after."

"So the day after. Did she give any indication that she was thinking of doing something…unusual?"

"No," he says.

Jackson leans forward in his chair. "Was she acting strangely?"

"No. If anything, she seemed calmer than usual."

"But David," says Frankenheimer, "isn't that a classic indication of some kind of decision or resolution outside the box?"

"It can be. But this was in the wake of an unusual event. She could have been in shock. I was looking for something in her that had been triggered. I couldn't find it."

"And she didn't say anything about wanting to leave?" Jackson asks.

"No. Sarah didn't want to leave here. She checked herself in. As a matter of fact, we were working on why she felt she needed to be here."

"And why did she?"

David looks at his shoes. "I can't answer that."

Jackson says, "Did she ever mention this other inmate? Excuse me, patient? Willie Cranston?"

"No."

"You didn't realize they knew each other?"

"No."

Jackson turns to Frankenheimer. "Did you ever see them socializing?"

"I don't walk the floors here, Detective."

He turns back to David. "Did you?"

"No. Ms. Lange mostly keeps to herself."

Jackson stares at his notebook and finally looks up. "Does she have any family nearby?"

"She doesn't have any family at all," David says.

"According to her."

"That's all I have to go on."

"But you have no reason to think she was lying about that?"

David says, "I have a sense that Ms. Lange doesn't know how to lie at all."

"But she is psychotic. People like that might not know the difference."

"She is not psychotic. I haven't had time to make a complete diagnosis but I have ruled out psychosis."

Jackson nods. He says, "Without asking you to betray any confidentiality, and keeping in mind that she has stolen a vehicle and kidnapped a patient, and both of their lives might be in danger, could you give me a vague idea of her diagnosis? As far as you've gotten, that is."

David thinks about answering. He understands what's at stake and he wants to help but every standard of integrity in his being fights a response.

He forms his words carefully. "She has Post Traumatic Stress Disorder. I can tell you that because it's a matter of public record. She was the victim of a violent crime a few years ago and participated in a police report. At that time, the medical records were submitted into evidence."

"I see. And in your experience, how does PTSD present?"

"You're a cop. A first responder. Surely you're no stranger to the condition."

"Surely I'm not. But I'm asking your professional opinion."

"It presents in a number of ways. None of them psychotic."

Jackson nods and flips his book closed.

"So we're back at square one."

"I suppose," David says. "I wasn't here for the first square."

"It's a complete mystery. To you and everyone who knew her."

David takes a long moment to think, staring at the carpet. What had Sarah said? Nothing in particular. Nothing of any substance. All he can recall is how much she hadn't wanted to see him that day, how much she hadn't wanted to talk.

Then something swims up to the surface of his brain. Some comment about being able to see her way through. Some reason for living she had recently located. He looks up and he knows his face betrays him. Frankenheimer sees it first.

"What?" she asks.

He wants to shut up but he feels caught.

"She told me," he says, "that she was starting to see a reason to be here."

"Here?" Jackson asks. "At Oceanside?"

"No, here. In the world. I took it as a sign."

"What kind of sign?"

"That she was feeling better. That she was moving away from the thought of suicide."

"She was suicidal?"

David feels caught again and embarrassed.

"She talked about it. A lot of patients do. We didn't consider her high risk in this environment," he says.

"I see." Jackson writes.

Frankenheimer stares hard at David. She is putting it together.

"So she had devised a plan," she says.

"No. I didn't take it that way."

"How did you take it?"

"Simply," he says. "As if we were making progress."

Frankenheimer says, "Dr. Sutton, don't you know better than to take your patients' revelations simply? Often when a suicidal patient becomes suddenly and inexplicably happy, it means they have devised a plan. Often a plan to commit suicide."

"It wasn't that way. It didn't feel that way. I know how to recognize that."

"But you didn't recognize this," Jackson says.

David turns his eyes squarely on the detective. "No. I am not trained to recognize when someone is planning to steal a truck and kidnap a fellow patient."

"Easy now," Jackson says.

David sighs, collecting what's left of his composure. Frankenheimer crosses her arms and narrows her eyes at him like a prosecutor. "So you are telling me that nothing she said indicated that she was about to make some kind of radical move."

"That's what I am telling you."

"Perhaps you were distracted. Because of what happened with Jen?"

"Dr. McCrady. No. No, my worlds don't mix."

Jackson issues a quiet laugh into his fist. "Teach me how to do that sometime. To keep your worlds from mixing. My wife would be interested to hear that."

"I don't believe we were discussing your wife," David says.

"No," Jackson says. "I'd better shut up about that or I'll owe you some money."

David doesn't smile.

Jackson leans in again. "I suppose what I want to know, what the family of Willie Cranston will want to know, is if you think she's violent?"

"No, I do not."

"And you aren't willing to elaborate?"

"No, I am not."

"We can subpoena her records," Jackson says. "Do you want us to go through that ordeal?"

"If you feel it's necessary."

Jackson offers his palms to the ceiling. "So we'll go through that ordeal. Meantime, your patient is probably crossing state lines with her victim. That makes it a felony. The Feds? They don't give two shits about psychological disturbance. They don't make deals. If you want to help her, I'm your last stop."

"I understand that."

Jackson stares at him, considering his next move. David decides to beat him to it.

"Am I free to go now, Detective?" he asks.

"Sure thing, Doc."

David walks to the door, trying to disguise how much he is shaking. His lack of control makes him ashamed but no one comments on it and the next thing he knows he is out of the corridor and into the parking lot and safely in his car. The uniformed cops are pacing the parking lot, smoking and laughing.

He has not had time to process the fact that Sarah is gone, traveling the dark highways in a stolen truck with some mental patient. He has not had time to process that he has failed her. Most of all, he has not had time to process that he will miss her and that on some level he feels he has been rejected and abandoned, like some high-school boy with a dangerous crush.

CHAPTER NINETEEN

Here's how it started.

I watched the space where they were sitting from the common room for a long time, watching the rain wash away their phantom images, and then the rain finally stopped and a rainbow came out over a corner of the ocean. I could see it from the common room but I wanted to see it better. I went out into the garden and stood and smoked, looking at the ocean, which unfolded beyond an expanse of grass on the Malibu hill.

So I was smoking and staring at the rainbow when a door burst open and Emily rushed into the courtyard, pacing and breathing, mumbling to herself. She didn't see me at first and when she did, her whole demeanor changed. Gone was her slightly unhinged affect, and in its place was a strong, stable woman struggling to overcome a moment of weakness.

"Sorry," she said.

"It's okay."

"I just need a little air before I go home."

"Sure," I said. "Did you see the rainbow?"

She looked in that direction and her breath caught. She put a hand to her chest. "Oh. That's so cool."

"Yeah," I said.

"You must think I'm crazy."

I laughed.

She recovered quickly. "No, I don't mean crazy. Just unstable."

"I barely notice that kind of thing around here."

She looked around her as if she had lost something tangible.

"I need to sit," she said, but all the benches were wet.

I whipped off a scarf I was wearing and said, "Here."

"Oh, no, don't."

But it was too late. I had wiped down the garden bench. She thanked me and sat.

I sat next to her.

"I was visiting my husband," she said.

"I know."

"You know?"

"Willie. We're in sewing class together."

"Oh," she said, momentarily cheered. And then her face dropped a little and she was worried. "Sewing?"

"Well, he treats it like art."

She nodded. "He's an artist."

"Was?"

"No, is. Is. Just because he's going through something doesn't mean his whole identity is wiped out."

"Yeah, I get that. I've seen his work. It's actual art. The rest of us are just fucking around."

She nodded, wiping her nose on the sleeve of her jacket.

She looked at me. "What do you do?"

"Do?"

"I mean, yeah."

"I was an artist, too."

"Really?"

"No, not really. Not like Willie. I write some. I do graphic design. Well, that's what I did. Right now I'm busy being crazy."

"Tell me about it," she said.

I knew I didn't have to tell her about it. We sat in silence and then I lit another cigarette. I offered her one but she shook her head.

"You're so pretty," she said.

"Well, thanks. You're pretty cute yourself."

"Oh. Well. I don't know."

"Don't worry. I'm not gay."

"I wasn't worried about that."

"I'm not even crazy."

She smiled. "I guess no one in here thinks they are crazy."

"Except Willie," I said. "He seems pretty reconciled to being crazy."

"No, he's really not. He was fairly stable for a long time. I mean, sure, he's bipolar. Manic depressive. Or something. We've always known that."

"Always?"

"Well, I knew it when I married him."

"When was that?"

"When we were twenty."

"Geez."

"I know, right? Who gets married that young?"

"When did you meet?"

"In college. At the University of Chicago. I was in business. He was an artist."

"Okay."

"But this was after he got out of the Navy."

"He was in the Navy?"

She nodded. "He was a Navy Seal. He had to drop out because of an injury. But he wanted to be an underwater mine specialist."

"What is that?"

"Someone who defuses mines. Underwater."

"Sounds dangerous."

She nodded. "He likes danger."

"He doesn't seem to like danger anymore."

"He's different now."

"Since the shock treatments?"

She looked at me as if I had seen into her soul. I was not trying to see into her soul.

"He told you that?" she asked.

"Yes."

"He's not supposed to talk about it. That was the agreement when we decided to do it. That he wouldn't talk about it."

"Yeah, but he forgot about the agreement?"

She nodded. "They told us there would be memory loss. But until that happens, you don't know what it means. I thought, oh, he'll forget our anniversary but he does that anyway. No one tells you how deep it goes. And no one tells you how much of your life together is actually based on memory. They keep saying it'll get better."

"But it's not better?"

She shook her head and stared at the ground.

After a moment she said, "It's sad. It's pathetic. But what else could we do?"

"I don't know. What else did you think about doing?"

She raised her eyes to me. She said, "I lived with this for years. We moved to L.A. so he could be a director. Or a photographer. Something with art. And he had some success. But every time he had success he would get depressed like this. He would talk about suicide. What was I supposed to do?"

"I don't know."

"Then one night he called me from the parking lot of a strip club."

"Jumbo's Clown Room. It's burlesque, not strip."

She smiled. "He told you that?"

"Yes."

"He had gone there with some guys. I try to give him a wide berth, you know? But he called me from there and said he wanted to jump off a bridge. I came and got him and then we ended up at County and then they sent us to Irvine to this doctor who was a big believer in ECT. It'll be bad for a while, he said, but then his brain will be reset and he'll be as good as new."

"That hasn't happened?"

She shook her head. "That hasn't happened yet."

The rainbow had disappeared and a voice came on the intercom calling all us crazies to our rooms.

"You should go, I guess," she said.

"Tell me," I said. "Tell me what you think went wrong in Jumbo's Clown room?"

"I don't know," she said. "I don't want to know. My job is to take care of him. That's my job. I married him knowing how he was. Some people have houses and children. I have him."

I narrowed my eyes at her. "You're a numbers person?"

She straightened up, swimming out of her emotional pool.

"I'm a financial analyst," she said. "For a software company."

"So you like numbers."

"I guess," she said.

"Numbers make sense."

She stared at me for a while. Finally she stood.

"I've taken up too much of your time," she said. "Thank you."

And then she walked with fixity of purpose to the door that took her away from all of us and back to the world that added up.

I thought on all of that for a long while, in my room, in the common room, in arts and crafts, at mealtime, wandering around in the garden. And I was formulating a theory as I strolled. Sometimes I could see Willie when I was making my rounds and sometimes I couldn't. The voices tried to pitch in but I shut them down.

All of this was happening to me, in real time, the way things happen to real people in the linear world. Events adding up, like numbers in a column, creating sums, making sense. The past influencing the present, the present making sense of the past, the future spreading out like the bricks and mortar of a new building waiting to take shape and all we had to do was the work.

What was reverberating in my brain, though, was that ridiculous passage that Dr. Sutton had read to me during our last session. The thing that Joseph Campbell had said. About artists being true revolutionaries. About how their jobs were to penetrate the social mask. About how they had to overcome the lower impulse of others to spill blood on the pavement to create yet another false mask. Or something like that.

And then he related it to my coming back from the other side. To do something like that. I had never asked myself that question but suddenly I was asking it and answering it at the same time. I had come back to recognize that impulse in others. To rescue it. To set loose the revolutionary whose job it was to save us from the false mask. This is why I found myself in such an unlikely place. This is why I met Willie when I did, in sewing class, witnessing him trying to create art. And he was being restrained and subdued because he was trying to demolish the social mask.

I knew what had occurred in the parking lot of Jumbo's Clown Room. Discharged from the Navy, married too young, art abandoned, looked after by his numbers-conscious wife, suddenly thrust into a room of thumping music and half-naked girls, it had occurred to him. He had lost his courage.

As if I needed another sign, the truck had been sitting there, keys in the ignition.

"So where are we going again?" Willie asked.

He let himself be led. He watched as I loaded his belongings on the floorboard around his feet.

"North."

"North of what?" he asked.

"North of here."

"Cool," he said.

Now he asks again. "Where are we going?"

"North," I tell him again. We are several hours into North. I wonder if anyone has missed us. I check the mirrors for lights or suspicious vehicles but don't see any.

"Cool," he says again.

CHAPTER TWENTY

David hears nothing more from Oceanside. That night he's worried enough to call his lawyer, Gerald Reigert, another friend from his days at Loyola. Gerald does whatever he wants for free because David didn't turn him in for cheating on a final exam there. Gerald is a very successful corporate attorney with an office in Beverly Hills but he still feels somehow that David could derail his whole life by posting a blog about Gerald's unsanctioned cheat sheet during senior physics.

"I owe you, man," Gerald says every time he picks up the phone.

"You don't owe me, Gerald," David says every time in response.

"No, listen, I know about paying the piper."

"You're not even Catholic," David reminds him on occasion.

"My mother is but what's your point? I'm a Jewish guy who went to Catholic school? That makes me doubly guilty."

On this occasion, David decides not to look a gift horse in the mouth. He listens to Gerald's counsel, not worrying about the bill.

"Dude, they got nothing on you," Gerald says. "Shrinks are so protected. You could practically kidnap someone yourself and I would take your case pro bono."

"Well, I don't want you to do that. I just want to be sure I'm okay."

"You're okay. Although, I have to tell you, lately? The medical world? You guys are superexposed. Shrinks are still pretty safe but everybody else? Give one guy a bottle of Valium and he hits somebody on the freeway and boom! You're on the stand."

"I try not to prescribe drugs."

"Yeah, but that's a whole other ball of wax. You don't prescribe drugs and the guy takes a shotgun to the shopping mall? Boom. On the stand."

"I thought you said I was okay."

"Oh, yeah, in this one you're okay. Just be careful."

He hangs up and calls Melinda Frankenheimer again.

He says, "I was just thinking. Willie Cranston's wife. Do you have a number for her?"

"It's confidential."

"You were all too ready to surrender my confidential files."

"Don't be that way, David."

"Don't you think it might help to call her?"

"We've spoken with her, believe me."

"I mean, if I called her."

"Why you?"

"Because Sarah is my patient."

"I don't understand. What would you possibly say to her?"

"I'd just let her know that I'm concerned and I'm in the fight."

"The fight?"

"To get him back. To get both of them back."

"I don't know. Sounds like a lawsuit waiting to happen."

"Actually, I think not reaching out would be more of a lawsuit."

There's a long silence and finally Melinda gives him the number.

"David, be careful. You were not exactly a silver-tongued devil with Detective Jackson."

"He's an authoritarian prick."

"Well, don't mince your words."

"Sarah is not a criminal. She's sick. The guy lacks compassion and what's more, I don't think he really cares about finding them. It was all for show. You probably won't hear from him again."

She sighs. "Well, that wouldn't be the worst thing in the world. For all of this to go away. I'll buy the gardener a new truck. And I'm sure we'll have to give a little compensation to Mrs. Cranston. You said Sarah Lange doesn't have any family?"

David breathes against his anger.

"I'm sure the blowback is your domain, Dr. Frankenheimer. Mine is caring for patients. So I'll do my part and you do yours."

"I envy you," she says. "I remember when that was all I had to do."

He hangs up on her. It's a luxury of the cell-phone age, never having to answer for a hang-up. Cut off. Lost service. In the old days, hanging up was a profound form of communication, hitting someone without making physical contact. He misses it.

He sits looking at Emily's number for a long time. Finally he dials it, thinking he has the option to hang up as soon as he hears her voice. But he immediately reaches voice mail. She sounds cheerful and high functioning. Her message says, "Hi, it's Emily, leave a message, thanks."

He doesn't leave a message.

CHAPTER TWENTY-ONE

The Ventana Inn is a hotel on the side of a cliff in Big Sur. Everything in Big Sur is on the side of a cliff. It is a cliff town. The drive up the narrow winding roads are harrowing at the best of times and downright nerve-racking in an old truck with a guy on Lithium driving. But it was something he needed to do. It's all part of the plan. Not my plan, either. I look out the window at the wild ocean, which looks anything but Pacific, and I have visions of plummeting and the vision doesn't disturb me but I also know this is not what's going to happen.

Big Sur has long been a siren call for dropouts, the most famous here being Henry Miller for which a library and museum is named. It is near Esalen, the cliffside self-enlightenment mecca that drew (ironically) Joseph Campbell every year on his birthday along with anyone with even a passing interest in hallucinogens. I had visited once many years ago. I signed up for a yoga retreat and had to sleep in a room with other yogis and work in the garden and basically be peaceful and contributing and I lasted three days. It was part of my plan to like people more. I didn't care much for them back in the day because I didn't understand that I was different; I thought they were all being recalcitrant and ignorant. I didn't understand they were doing their part. They were listening to their own voices. And I needed to listen to mine.

So I really didn't get yoga the first time around and I had fantasies of driving stakes into people's hearts whenever they said namaste and I was quite a nasty little intellectual before that nice young man killed me. My fiancé and I were already broken up then but we never would have survived my conversion. He is still a nasty little intellectual. Cranky, road raging, ranting, sour in his affect, glaring at the news of the world. Of course I don't know this but I know this. I don't astrally visit him or anything so this is more of an assumption than a vision. Sometimes you just know how people are without knowing how people are. We call it something else. We call it, "I know what I know."

Willie does not seem afraid to be driving up the winding road and in fact seems comforted by the fact that he has but one thing to think about. When we make it to the top he doesn't seem surprised or impressed with himself. That might be because he's not a hundred percent sure of where he is or what he is doing or even who I am. I don't talk to him at all until it's time to turn into the Ventura Inn and then I only say, "Turn here." And he does.

Once we're in the parking lot I wait while he smokes a cigarette and gets his bearings.

"This is cool," he says.

"Yes."

"Big trees."

"Yes."

"Reminds me of Oregon."

"You've been to Oregon?"

"I'm from there. I grew up on a farm."

"You remember that."

"Sure. It's mostly short-term stuff that I have trouble with."

"Right."

"Like...where are we?"

"In Big Sur."

"Did I know that before?"

"I mentioned it when we left."

"Wait, we left?"

"Yes, we left the hospital."

"I was in a hospital?"

This news seems to alarm him the most.

"Well, no, it's really a rehab center."

He has no idea what to make of that. I wait and his eyes scan the ground and then he lifts his head and says, "Oh, yeah."

"Yeah."

Now I can see another question tumbling in his brain but it's having trouble getting out.

"Emily?" I suggest.

"Yes. Where's Emily?"

"Back home."

"What do I tell her?"

"Whatever you want."

"But I don't know what we're doing."

"You'll know when we're done."

"Okay." He grinds out his cigarette and puts his hands in his pockets and sighs. "It's pretty here."

The woman at the desk has almost no reaction to us, a dazed giant and his diminutive companion. In Big Sur, I'm sure we are barely noticeable. She's a little disturbed that we don't have a reservation but is happy to tell us there's a deluxe room available and even happier when my credit card gets approved. We register as Mr. and Mrs. Jack Rabbit and that doesn't interest her very much, either.

"Thank you, Mrs. Rabbit. Jorge is waiting outside with a cart to take you to your room. Enjoy your stay."

Willie enjoys the golf cart ride to the room very much. It makes him grin. Jorge is telling us all about the things we are passing but we don't listen.

Big Sur is not a relaxing beachfront place. It's an edge-of-the-world beachfront place. Our hotel seems perched on the precipice of sudden understanding. Our front yard is a cliff overlooking crashing waves. It's like a live action version of the covers of romance novels. All that's missing is a woman in Victorian garb and a cape whipped by the ruthless wind. And somewhere in the background, a man who has done her wrong in silent pursuit with the devil nipping at his heels.

The sun is going down as we go into our large room with a wood-burning fireplace and a patio and a hammock. Willie lowers himself into the hammock and stares at the ocean until it disappears into blackness.

I sit in front of the fire and stare at it until I begin to feel sleepy, then I call Willie in because the night has gotten cold. He had fallen asleep in the hammock and when he wakes up it takes a long time for him to get his bearings and I have to tell him all over again where we are and why. Then he says, "It's freezing out here."

"I made a fire."

He sinks in the armchair and stares into the fire the way that I was doing and I don't sit down beside him with a book because I am afraid it will make me feel too much like we're married and that would confuse him even more. And would confuse me, too. This was my favorite way to spend time with my fiancé when we were together. We lived in England then, the early days. To keep the heating bill down we'd turn it off at night and he would build a fire and we would sit in front of it with our books. Mine usually some turn-of-the-century respectable piece of English or American literature and his some history tome about Nelson or Byron or Bletchley Park. We would sit there with such purpose. Staying warm, broadening our minds, being peaceful, being close. To this day I can't imagine why that stopped being enough for us. I want to say it was him but I'm sure I started to drift around the time he did. What did we need to replace us? In his case, he needed another woman, a lawyer it turned out, who didn't read books for pleasure at all, just worked all the time. I can't let myself think about what he found in her that was missing in me. Back when I had friends, I had this friend named Laurie who used to say, "He didn't find anything, Sarah, he just moved on to the next warm body when you left."

I am remembering my friends. This must be some aspect of recovery.

Laurie had shoulder length curly hair and crystal blue eyes. She sang. For a living? No, just for fun. She taught for a living. And then there was Samantha. She had short brown hair, a pixie cut, and saucer eyes. Her smile took up her whole face. She was a dog trainer. Did they have husbands? Did they have children? What did we talk about? I can't remember those details. I am starting to remember their voices. Chattering, like the heavens chatter, saying things that mattered and didn't matter and filling up the room like music.

All of my friends were analytical, as I was, and most of them funny, as I was, and everything that happened to us somehow seemed to be occurring in a movie or a play or a respectable turn of the century novel. We had no idea it was all a tawdry pretense, utter, calamitous, chaotic nonsense. We thought we were building something. We thought it was smart.

Maybe it was smart. Maybe we did matter and maybe we were building something. I can't remember. I feel it tugging at me like some irksome task I need to return to. I shake my head to rid myself of it.

But I can't rid myself of it. I see Laurie, crying, sitting on the edge of my bed.

"You were always the strong one," she said.

What did she mean? Was it a criticism? Was it some kind of plea?

"I can't stand this," Samantha said.

Why did she say that?

I see myself lying in a bed, the two of them sitting on the edge of it, crying. Am I in the hospital?

Yes, it is a memory, and I am in the hospital and my two friends are trying to talk to me. I have just come back from the dead and I'm trying to focus on my life now that I'm back in it. I see the way my two friends are looking at me. Relieved that I'm back from the dead but at the same time, afraid of me. Disgusted by me? Feeling like I'm somehow altered? Dirty and broken? Maybe I'm imagining that.

And then I see myself walking around my apartment, my phone in my hand, wondering whom to call. Then I hear the voices. Not in my head, in the room. Someone talking to me. Not Samantha, not Laurie. Disconnected voices.

Yes, they left me. My friends left me. They tried to hang around for a while but then they left and then the radio started playing in my head. Then I dropped to my knees and demanded the disconnected voices identify themselves.

This story, the way I used to tell it, always felt purposeful and heavenly. Now it's coming back to me and I'm looking at it as if I'm behind a tattered curtain and I'm starting to see a hurt and frightened girl, alone with her injuries, replacing lost voices with imagined voices.

But I couldn't have imagined those voices. My imagination is not that good.

Suddenly I am back in the room in Big Sur. I can smell the smell of the fireplace.

Instead of sitting next to Willie I go into the bathroom and draw a bath and I sit in that and am very happy. They don't let us take baths at Oceanside. Maybe the addicts can but I think with the crazies, there's too long of an association with baths and suicide. I don't know why they think we can't kill ourselves in a shower. As I'm thinking of this, I realize I have to correct my tense because I am not in Oceanside anymore and I have no idea if I'm ever going back.

Even though I'm happy about my bath and satisfied with my mission, I am starting to feel a little unsafe and riled up. I try to push that feeling down but it won't push. Then I try to pretend it's about something else, like a difficult trip and tiredness and being out of my element or even thinking about my fiancé and my friends and my old life. But I know what it is.

The voices have gone.

Not fluctuating the way they did before, which was really more like getting louder and fainter, but even when I couldn't hear them I could feel them. Since we left Oceanside, though, I can't even feel them. I am starting to feel the way I did in my old life. Grounded. Sensible. Sure. Mean. Frustrated. I know what Dr. David Sutton would call this feeling. He would call it cured.

CHAPTER TWENTY-TWO

Jen has found a doctor who has put her on antianxiety meds and now she is less loud but still anxious. Only a few days have passed since the incident but David can see that the drugs have taken an edge off the meanness. Now the meanness is less interesting, less entertaining. Or maybe he is making it that way because he is wedded to his antimedication philosophy. Doctors become so invested in their methodologies, to abandon them is like a divorce and he doesn't want to get a divorce or even a separation. With his girlfriend drifting away from him and his most important patient on the run, David is thrashing around for any port in the storm.

He is finding it difficult to anchor himself to his anorexics and bulimics and he wonders why his practice has turned into this. For a long time he was the go-to guy for serious disorders. He was on a steady diet of severe phobics, PTSDs, OCDs, suicidal ideations, drug-resistant bipolars, a few delusionals, and one schizophrenic. Now he finds himself listening to young adults talking about the circumstances that cause them to abuse food, sex, substances, and sharp objects. They've drifted to him under the umbrella of PTSD but their disturbances really have little to do with trauma. What they are labeling trauma is often just discordance. Assholes for parents. Vampires for friends. Lazy demi-gods for teachers. He knows how to help someone step through the aftermath of genuine trauma—a violent crime, a debilitating accident of some kind. But he feels entirely unqualified to guide someone through the basic machinations of life. He doesn't have a clue about why it all unfolds as it does. He understands hate and despair and bullying and free-ranging rage. He understands them as energies that everyone taps into from time to time. He just doesn't understand them as a dedicated path, a system, a way of moving in the world.

So what can he say to these children? How can he tell them it is going to get better when, in his experience, it doesn't? Bullies become psychopaths who just put on suits and develop a more personable demeanor. The needy just glamorize their need, call it seduction and romance. The outcasts find each other and develop a lair of alienation, sometimes turning it into art, more often turning it into bitterness or violence. The world, he wants to tell his children, does not get better, it just gets bigger. You will find others like yourself. You will have a band, a gang, a klatch. But your band or gang or klatch will still be poised to do battle against your tormentors. The brave ones will take that on. The gentler ones will retreat and stay in the shadows together.

The world is brutal, children. The mode is brutality. The commonwealth is a smoke screen. Underneath the advertisement, a festering war.

Dear God, who is having these thoughts? It can't be him. Something is possessing him.

He is sitting in front of the small fireplace in his study, even though it is a very warm evening, because he wants to look into the fire, because he feels something in common with combustion right now.

It's not that he hasn't always seen the darker side of human nature. But he used to have a clearer view of the other side of that. He felt balance, even if the scale more often tipped against the light. But he never felt these things with any degree of passion. It's the volume of his thoughts that disturb him more than their content.

He has never sought passion. He has always felt grateful for the lack of it. He is an epicurean by nature. Contrary to common mythology, an epicurean is one who takes moderate pleasure in all things. Epicurus was not a binger. He was a taster. And that's how he always saw himself, as one who could and did take moderate bites of the good and the bad, never letting any of them race out of control. Now he is being swept away with strong notions.

A passion is forming. A devotion is pulling ahead and dragging him with it.

And it isn't just a concept. It's a feeling in his body. His stomach churns. He is light-headed. His heart races then slows to what feels like a stop. He fears he is becoming a crusader but he doesn't have a crusade. He doesn't know what he is for. He only knows what he is against and that has just started to come into focus. He would never be able to put it down as a dissertation. It's just a vague idea that the world is out of joint. As a scientist he has struggled all his life against positionality. Now it is creeping up on him like an infection invading his body.

"What are you doing?"

It is Jen's even but stern voice. He jumps.

"Nothing. Thinking."

"It's a million degrees. A fire? Really?"

"Do you need something?"

She hands him his phone. "It's been ringing a lot. Are you on call?"

"No."

"I didn't mean to pry. I didn't recognize the name."

He takes the phone and looks at the voice mail. Three calls from Emily Cranston.

His heart lurches. "Oh."

"Who is Emily Cranston?"

"She's the wife of a patient."

Jen lifts her hands in surrender. "Never mind."

"It's complicated."

"It sounds that way."

"Jen."

"It's okay. I have to get back to work."

She walks away. This is how she is now. Quietly judgmental. There is an evenness to her disdain.

David's hand shakes a little as he calls Emily back. She doesn't pick up. While he is stumbling over a message, a call from her comes in. He answers it.

"Sorry," she says, "I just missed the call. I was in a loud place. I'm okay now."

His head is spinning. "Yes, I..."

"Sorry about the last message. I was just getting a little worked up."

"I actually didn't listen to your messages. I was eager to get in touch with you."

"You didn't seem eager to get in touch with me. You called me once and didn't leave a message."

"How did you…"

"I saw the number on my phone and dialed it. I heard your message, I Googled you, I called Oceanside and I found out you were treating that psychopath who kidnapped my husband."

"Yes. I was treating her. We had only had a few sessions."

"What is wrong with her?"

"I hadn't gotten to the bottom of that. And even if I had…"

"I know, you can't tell me. I have a crazy husband. I know how you people work."

"Have you heard from him?"

"No."

"Do you have any idea where he might have gone?"

"I don't think he's the one planning the vacation."

"But let's just say that he is part of it somehow."

"Dr. Sutton, my husband can barely decide what to have for breakfast. If you had known him, you'd be aware that there is no way he could have schemed anything. Besides, I talked to her so I know how she is."

"And how is that?"

"She was getting information from me. She tricked me."

"What kind of information?"

"She got me to open up about Willie's situation. I told her stuff."

"What kind of stuff?"

"Just how it happened and how I felt about it."

"How what happened?"

"The breakdown. Should we really try to accomplish this on the phone?"

"No, of course not. We can meet."

"I'm in Hollywood."

"I'm in Venice. But I'll come to you."

"Meet me at the Standard Hotel. Do you know where that is?"

"Yes."

"Oh, a shrink with a secret clubbing life."

He laughs. "Hey, hipsters go crazy, too."

"Good point."

He tells Jen he is leaving. She has a simmering reaction.

"You're going to meet your patient's wife?"

"He's not actually a patient. It's a long story."

"You're going to meet some woman somewhere right now? I was going to make dinner."

He inhales deeply and looks at his watch.

"You heard about the kidnapping at Oceanside? That was my patient, Sarah Lange. This is the wife of the guy she kidnapped."

Jen stares at him as if the whole story is too much for her drug-quieted mind. Her old mind would have had torrents of opinions on this. But now she just blinks at him. Then she gives a dismissive wave.

"Fine."

"I don't know how late…"

"Fine."

He means to walk out but finds he can't. "Jen, do you think the drugs are really helping?"

"Is this the start of an antidrug campaign?"

"No, it's a real question."

She stares at the fire and thinks.

"How do I know if they're helping?" she asks. "My doctor will tell me if they're helping."

"But how do you feel?"

She stares at the fire again.

"I feel like every ounce of energy in me is being used to hang on."

"Hang on to what?"

"I don't know."

The answer defuses his impulse to go deeper. What he was cooking up was petty and strange. He wants to take her on. He wants to argue about commitment and love. He wants to ask what they are doing. He wants to dismantle the whole thing right here and now. But he knows that it is avoidance, that the real conflict is waiting for him at the Standard Hotel and parts unknown.

"Will you be all right if I leave?" he asks.

"No less all right than when you're here," she says.

He lets her have the last word.

CHAPTER TWENTY-THREE

The Ventana Inn has a clothing-optional as well as a clothing-required pool area. They both include hot tubs and the ones in clothing optional are much nicer so it's clear which way they want you to go. It is too cold for swimming but I think it might be good for us to sit in the hot tubs and we might as well use the nice ones; I just have to pray that no naked girls decide to join us because I'm not sure how Willie will respond to that. Given that the last time he saw nearly naked girls who weren't his wife he ended up driving himself to shock treatments.

We walk down to the clothing-optional pools, wearing bathrobes over our institutional swimwear. Mine is a Speedo one-piece and I'm not sure what Willie's is. I just told him to put on a bathing suit and he came out of the bathroom in a robe and slippers. I slept the night in a chair in front of the fire and Willie took over the bed. Before he went to sleep, he constructed an elaborate village of pillows. When I saw his sleep environment in the morning I said, "Does NASA know about this? Because I think you could sell it to them."

He just blinked at me and said, "I have back issues."

He didn't ask me about where we were or what were doing. He just followed orders and now he is following me down the winding path to the clothing-optional pool. We are surrounded by exaggerated trees. We are in a kind of fort. I act like I know what I'm doing. But now that the voices have stopped, I have no idea what I am doing. I am trying to cling to a sense of purpose. I know that Willie was dying a slow death at Oceanside and I am somehow rescuing him. But I also know that by doing so, I have catapulted us into some kind of outlaw status. People might be looking for us. We might be hiding. I might be in trouble of some kind. When I made this decision, I was very sure of myself. Now I feel cut loose from that. I am trying to devise a plan. I am dancing as fast as I can. I have two problems now. I am divorced from my guidance and I am in charge of a man who is hardly there. I can see him coming back a little. He has been off the Lithium for a day. I expect he will emerge as a person a little over time. I don't exactly know what I'll do with him when he fully lands. Right now he is still shuffling, waiting to be led.

This might be the first time I've fully registered how huge he is. He is a foot taller than I am. He seems completely unaware of this fact. He moves like someone who knows he takes up a lot of space but has no idea what to do about it.

He rubs his head as we approach the clothing-optional pool.

"Man," he says. "I slept really hard last night."

"Me, too," I say, thought I hadn't slept hard. I had dozed in front of the fire and woke up about once an hour.

"What are we doing now?" he asks.

"We're visiting the hot tubs."

"I like hot tubs."

"Me, too."

The clothing-optional pool is devoid of customers. We walk through the changing rooms and the sauna area and finally we arrive at the hot tubs. We step into them gingerly. The warm water engulfs us. It feels like being hugged. I sink down to my chin. Willie observes me and sinks down the same way, though he has to collapse his legs to a kneeling position. We exist there for a moment, not looking at each other.

"Where are we?" he asks.

"In Big Sur."

"What is that?"

"It's a place in Northern California."

"Why?"

"Why what?"

"Why are we here?"

"Well, we needed to get out of town."

"Okay."

We float for another minute more. He turns his head and the turning of his head seems to take a great deal of effort. He looks at my face and then he stares at my chest. It is underwater but he can still see. He stares at the top of my cleavage. My chest is mostly covered up by my choice of a professional swimsuit. Yet he still seems to see something.

"I'm not with you, right?" he asks.

"Well, you're with me but you're not really with me."

He thinks about that. He scratches his wild hair.

"Emily," he says.

"Yes," I say.

"Does she know where we are?"

"I'm not entirely sure."

"We should call her."

"We will."

We float in the water for a little while longer. Something corrosive is coursing through my veins. This is how I felt before I accepted the voices. I don't know what I'm doing. I'm just bouncing from one opportunity, one series of events to another. I react. I don't respond. I'm in control of nothing. It generates a feeling of panic in me. I have some distant idea that it was the realization that I was in control of nothing that made me give in to the voices and landed me in Oceanside. But now I feel some kind of willpower returning. I might have the privilege of choice. I might have the burden of choice. I might have to make a decision. I don't know what to do. I can feel Willie's eyes burning into some part of my skin. And it reminds me of how I felt right before I committed to the voices. I couldn't take it anymore. I couldn't stand being vulnerable to the way the world worked. All those base desires and needs and plans and outright evil. The evil of a man crawling through my window to humiliate me. It had unbearable weight. The randomness of it all burned holes in my skin. I wanted to fix it, the demise of the human condition, yet I couldn't even fix myself. I wasn't up to the task so I gave up the task. I welcomed the guides.

I am suddenly recalling my time at Oceanside, where I had nothing to do but confess, and after I had confessed, I stared out windows and sometimes I smoked. That seemed enough of a charge. Now I seem to have things to answer for. I might have to answer for bringing Willie here. I might be responsible for him. At Oceanside, I was responsible for nothing. I went from feast to famine. I hated having no influence on the world. I loved having no influence on the world. Here, I am in some kind of purgatory where I have some kind of effect but no kind of effect. I am somewhere between Newtonian physics (cause and effect) and Quantum physics (no kind of effect) and I feel as crazy as I have ever felt.

But I have to hide this from Willie who has developed a weird kind of intense stare as the Lithium wears off. Why had I ever thought he was Bambi? I have no idea what to do with him now.

I find myself missing Dr. David Sutton. I find myself endowing him with all kinds of mystical powers. Like he was a lion tamer. And I am the lion. A lion set loose from its environment. Not sure whether to kill or sleep. Equally interested in both ideas. Not overly invested in either. Something rises in me and it feels like fear and I haven't felt fear in a long time.

I got here by being sure of something. And the certainty has deserted me. I am a particle cut loose from gravity. Panic sweeps in on me. I am just a woman in a Speedo swimsuit in a hot tub next to an enormous man whose sense of calm is wearing off.

"Did I tell you about Jumbo's Clown Room?" he asks.

"Yes."

He nods and stares off, letting his legs float up. He stares at them.

The world feels peaceful but it is not peaceful.

"What did I tell you?" he asks.

"That you went there and you started to feel weird and then you called your wife and then you got shock treatments."

"Right," he says. He stares at his legs as if they aren't a part of him. I stare at them the same way.

What was I thinking?

"Should we get breakfast?" I ask.

He shakes his head. "I'm not hungry."

"Okay."

We float some more. All I can hear is the sound of the filter in the hot tubs and the sound of the motor churning the bubbles and there's really nothing natural about this. Panic grips my throat and I don't understand why and I search for the voices but they are gone.

To replace the sounds I say, "I think I understand. You saw these women. And maybe you wanted these women. But you lost your courage."

He looks at me as if I'm seriously disturbed. Maybe I am seriously disturbed. But he is, too. Two seriously disturbed people in a hot tub in Big Sur. What to do with that? He says, "I feel like my thinking is coming back to me."

"That's good. Right?"

"I don't know. I don't think my thinking is so good."

"Thinking is just thinking. It's not action."

"But thinking leads to action. Doesn't it? That's what the doctors say."

I don't answer. I look at my feet. They look old. I thought I was young. It's a lot of information at once.

He says, "Let me tell you what I was thinking in the parking lot of Jumbo's Clown Room."

"Okay."

"I was watching these women dancing. And did I want them? Yes, I wanted them. But that's not a big deal. Men just go around wanting other women. Women don't do that. Once they find a man, they just want that man."

"Often," I say.

"Why is that?" he asks.

"I guess it's DNA. It's caveman logic. And women in caveman times were just getting raped and beaten up all the time. Then we realized if we allied with one man, he would protect us. Women originally wanted one man so they could stop feeling threatened. But things have changed. We can buy weapons. But there is something in our cells that still makes us desire men for protection."

Willie digests this and asks, "What about love?"

"I guess on a cellular level we love you for protecting us."

Willie struggles to process this. Finally he says, "I was looking at those women and I started to feel mean."

"Okay."

"Not just mean."

"Okay."

"Dangerous," he says evenly.

"Dangerous how?"

He shrugs. The water lifts and gulps as his body moves.

"I wanted to kill them," he says simply.

"Oh," I say.

But I don't feel "oh." I feel panic sweeping over me. What am I doing? Why am I in a hot tub with this enormous man, whose hold on his darker side is diminishing the longer I keep him out of his protected environment. It's as if I'm with a tiger who has been tranquilized and the tranquilizer is wearing off.

"I really wanted to kill them," he repeats.

"Okay."

"I had visions of taking them, one by one, and choking them to death."

I don't know what to say. My skin is starting to wrinkle. I am feeling light-headed. I am hungry. I am suspended in this moment.

The sounds of the hot tub fill in some blanks but then the sounds of the motors drift away and I can hear the trees bowing in the wind and the ocean somewhere in the distance. We are in the wild. No one knows we are here.

He says, "Do you want to know why I wanted to kill them?"

"Sure."

I don't want to know why. I am unprepared to know why.

He says, "Because they are so simple. They think they are so simple. But they have this power. They know what they are doing. They are teasing us. They are mocking us. We are so much...I don't know how to describe it...we are so much less. I was a Navy Seal. I know how to kill a person with a punch to the throat. But killing a person is nothing. The strippers, they know how to torture a person. They know how to take that thing inside of you, that thing that haunts your sleep, that has the power to undo you, and they know how to use it against you, and make it come awake and deplete you."

"I've never heard you talk this much, Willie," I say, stalling for time.

"I can't remember talking this much. This is how I used to feel."

"How does it feel now?" My hands are shaking.

"It feels like real life."

"Does Emily know you feel this way?"

His face goes blank. He stares at the middle distance, his face stalled.

"Emily?" he asks.

"Your wife."

He turns his head to me and his eyes land on me and they are a little dead but much less dead.

"What does she have to do with this?" he asks.

"I don't know. Did you tell her any of this?"

He shrugs and the water burps again. "I can't really remember my life with her."

"Really."

"Yeah," he says. "The drugs do that. They make me forget my middle life. I remember everything before and everything after."

"We should probably get something to eat."

I start climbing the stairs out of the pool. He grabs my arm. It hurts but I trust he doesn't mean it to hurt. Men don't know their strength. Men don't know how fragile we are.

"Why are you walking out on me?" he demands.

"I'm not. I'm really not. But it's late morning and we're probably hungry."

"I don't want food."

"We forget to eat. Remember that from Oceanside? We forget to eat. That's why they put us on a schedule."

"What is Oceanside?"

"Let's go."

"What schedule? Where are we?"

"Never mind. We have to get out of the pool. We need to eat some protein."

I am afraid. His grip on my arm is hard. I feel the circulation cutting off.

"I didn't kill them, did I? The girls at Jumbo's. Did I kill them?" he asks.

"As far as I know, you've never killed anyone," I say.

He puts his face in his watery hands. He cries but it's a dramatic cry. I have no idea what I've taken on.

He finally looks up at me and his eyes are red from the chlorine.

He says, "On my father's farm. In Oregon. He took me out to shoot a cow. I was thirteen. He made me shoot the cow. I fired the gun and the cow fell. It didn't yell or make a sound. It just fell. One minute it was a cow and then it was nothing. I cried for three days."

"Okay."

"My father beat me. He called me weak."

"Okay."

"Taking a life. Any kind of life. You will never know."

"Okay."

Willie stares at the trees for a long moment. Finally he says, "Killing an animal is cowardly. Killing a cow is nothing. But killing a human? Courage has to be tested."

"Okay."

He grips my hand. "I have no courage."

"You're just repeating what I said."

"It's the truth."

"Maybe you have a different kind."

"Don't split words."

"I'm not. I'm hungry. Aren't you hungry?"

He looks at the bubbling water.

"I suddenly feel very heavy. Do you ever feel that way?"

"Half the time," I say.

"And the other half?"

"The other half? I feel fine."

I stand there in my point of crisis. I have no idea where I am or what I am doing. I have no idea how to proceed in the absence of the voices. And in the absence of them, I feel like a fraud and a failure. I blame them for not talking. I blame myself for not listening. Mostly I feel stranded in this terrible place of real life, where I have choice and logic and all that horrible stuff at my disposal.

"Let's go get breakfast," I say again.

He stares at me for what seems like a long time and finally he stands and the water comes up to his waist and he runs his hands through his hair.

"Okay, I could eat," he admits.

CHAPTER TWENTY-FOUR

Emily is sitting in a corner booth. She is wearing a cream-colored hoodie and she is staring at the drink in front of her—some kind of cocktail on ice—and she is uninterested in the stimuli around her. When David walks in she looks up and waves her chin at him, as if they are old friends. David moves toward her. He feels out of his element but he is aware that he feels out of his element anytime he leaves his comfortable surroundings. It's not as if he never visits Hollywood. But he usually does so in an entirely protected way. He visits Hollywood on professional consultations, sometimes with the Hollywood Free Clinic, sometimes on house calls to fancy hotels. The point is, he never enters Hollywood just as a person who lives in Los Angeles, and this is how he feels now. He has no real credentials as he enters the restaurant at the Standard Hotel. He feels like a fan, a tourist, someone who is scamming.

He immediately knows Emily. He recognizes her face from hearing her voice. She looks like someone who mostly smiles, but the smile has been ironed out of her skin. She is someone who is eternally optimistic but she has had the optimism temporarily knocked out of her. As he looks at her, he sees a kind of mask, a kind of provisional countenance. Jen would say she has positive energy. He tries not to think of Jen but as he looks at Emily, he feels the truth of this concept. There's an energy to Emily. It's impossible to deny it.

Emily doesn't stand or wave but she guides him to her table with her chin.

Her arms remain crossed. As he approaches her, she half stands and they shake and he sits across from her.

"Do you want a drink?" she asks immediately.

"No. Maybe. I don't know."

"I'm having a martini on the rocks," she says.

"Okay. I can have a scotch, I guess."

He seems to keep talking but she ignores him and waves down the waiter and he orders a scotch on the rocks and then he is looking at her again.

There is something about her. She is angry and happy and churned up and at peace all at once. He doesn't know what to make of her. He tries to analyze her. He can't. He is overwhelmed by her disparate energies.

"Okay, let's get to it," she says.

"Get to what?"

"Do you know where my husband is?" she asks.

"No. Of course I don't."

She looks at her lap. He takes a breath.

"Maybe we should start again," he says.

She leans over the table, folding her hands. "This isn't a Hollywood opening or a garden party. My husband is missing with a patient of yours. He's in danger. She's in danger. We have to figure this out."

"How are they in danger?"

Emily rolls her eyes. "I don't know about your patient. All I know about her is that she kidnapped my husband. But I will tell you this. He is dangerous."

"How so?"

Emily smiles and shakes her shiny brown hair away from her face.

"What do you people do? Do you really bother to get to know your patients?"

David clears his throat. "Your husband was not my patient. I don't know the first thing about him. My patient, Sarah Lange, is not dangerous."

"Except when she's kidnapping people."

"We don't have proof that she kidnapped him."

Emily waves his comment away. She stares into her drink, looks out the window, then looks back at him.

"Okay, lookit. I know Will. I've been married to him since I was twenty. I'm not twenty anymore, you might have guessed."

Emily is one of those ageless women. Her face is thirty and her demeanor is fifty and her age could be anywhere in between.

She says, "Look, I don't have kids. And my career isn't really a career. It's just a job. I support my husband. I knew he was disturbed when I married him. So his condition, for lack of a better word, is my child. I take care of him. That's what I do."

"Okay."

"But now your client has taken him away. Why?"

"All right, listen. Just because she's my client…patient…it doesn't mean she's an appendage of me. I don't understand her all that well. We were engaged in a process."

"Well," Emily says, "I don't care that much about her. Honestly, Harry Potter could have kidnapped my husband in his current state."

"What is his current state?"

"He is undergoing treatment. Shock treatment. It's extreme, I know. But you know why you take extreme measures? For extreme conditions."

David feels his head swimming from the scotch. A fog is moving in.

Emily leans across the table.

"My husband is dangerous," she says.

"Dangerous," David repeats. Most people talk about danger as if they know anything about it. They mostly don't. People mostly aren't dangerous, in his experience, the way others talk about it. Others are mostly talking about sarin gas in the subway or pipe bombs in high school. That happens rarely. Most people are only dangerous to themselves, which is a certain kind of danger, but the lesser kind.

Emily says, "Look, do you think I would have agreed to give my husband shock treatments if he were just kinda sad? What kind of person do I look like to you?"

She looks like a very nice, very controlled, very optimistic kind of person.

"Shock treatments?" David repeats.

"ECT."

"He is getting ECT treatments?"

"Yes."

"Why?"

"Because he requested them."

"Why?"

"Because he was sick of his head. I was sick of it, too. We tried every other thing."

David lets that information land though he has no idea what to do with it. He decides to return to the situation at hand.

"What makes you think he is dangerous?" he asks.

Emily takes a deep breath. She says, "I picked him up from the strip club that night. Jumbo's Clown Room. We sat in the car for a long time, talking about how he felt."

"Okay."

She leans over the table. There is some kind of disco music thumping from somewhere. Emily seems separate from it somehow, and yet distantly connected, as if it's a soundtrack to their conversation.

She says, "I'm sure he didn't mean to do what he did. It's not like him."

"What did he do?"

"He choked me. I don't think he knew he was doing it."

David wants to have a big reaction but he doesn't. His scientific brain has kicked in. He tries to keep a neutral expression. Her eyes are racing across the tabletop as if she's reading it. He knows she's remembering.

"What stopped him?" David asks.

She shrugs. "He just suddenly stopped. It was like he came out of a trance. I don't know how to say this. I'll just say it. It was like he was possessed."

David nods.

"And then?"

She shrugs again. "I drove him to the hospital and here we are."

David has his drink in front of him now and he's happy to concentrate on it.

"Did you ever think of leaving him?" he asks.

She looks at him, confused. "Why?"

"He was violent toward you."

"I told you, it wasn't really him."

"You don't actually believe in possession."

"No."

"So it was him."

"It was his disease."

"Do we know what that is exactly?"

"Bipolar Type II."

"Okay."

"Look, I am not happy being married to a crazy person. But I took a vow. And this woman who has him now? No vow. She has no idea what she's up against."

"Up against?"

"I have no idea what he's going to be like when the meds wear off. She might be in danger from me when we find her."

"Don't say that."

"She stole my mentally ill husband."

"She's mentally ill as well, Emily. I know it's hard but you have to show her the same compassion you do your husband."

He is disturbed by the way his heart is hammering, the way he can feel his face flushing. The need to defend Sarah is more than he can comprehend. And he is sure that it is showing on his face and that Emily is reading it. But she's not. She is staring beyond him, toward an impulse to cry.

He wants to tell her he will fix it. He wants to say he will make it all right. For the first time in his professional career he wants to go beyond what science is telling him. Science is telling him this is a big, dangerous mess. But he ignores that data for the sake of the woman sitting next to him and, in some regard, for the sake of himself.

"We are going to find them," he says. "It's going to be all right."

Emily leans against his shoulder. And now he knows he is in it.

CHAPTER TWENTY-FIVE

I take a walk among the giant trees in the gloaming. They are imposing, like bullies. I feel dwarfed and a little imprisoned by them. I feel like a character in a Grimm's fairy tale. I don't know why people find this atmosphere relaxing. But really it's just my state of mind. I appreciate the sounds of the space, a fluttering and a dripping and a silence so profound it sounds like a voice. It's that silence I want to be with. Because the silence is a voice. That's where God is. I have lost Him. I have lost the guides. I am the one who moved away and I don't know how I did that.

I sit on a bench. I have to think. No, I have to stop thinking. I have to listen. I have to wait.

Nothing fills the void.

I can't help thinking.

Joan of Arc. She stopped hearing the voices, too. Few people know this about the story. After she crowned the Dauphine, which was her original and only task, she continued to fight. She led her army into another village to eradicate the presence of the British. No one asked her to do that. It was her own plan. She was getting ahead of God. She decided she could take it from there. And this was why she was captured. If she had finished her task and gone home or waited for her next task, it might have gone differently. She wasn't executed for hearing voices or even going into battle. She was executed for wearing men's clothing. If she had agreed to stop they would have let her go. She died over wardrobe issues.

But not really. Really she died because she had fallen in love with her identity and could not give it up. She was brave and boisterous in her trials. She was sarcastic. She didn't bat an eye. It was an authority to whom she did not answer. She was convinced she was going to be released. By now she was having her visions again, though they didn't speak, just showed up to comfort her. They never told her she was going to be released but she assumed this. And when the trial kept going and her prospects looked bleak she began to panic and she railed against God. She attempted to escape by jumping out a window. She was slightly injured and recaptured.

The last few days before she was convicted, the visions came more consistently. And there's some indication that they told her to accept her fate. By the time they put her in the fire, she had surrendered to them and to her death, and there are reports that she was ecstatic in the fire. She was seeing Heaven.

I don't know how we can know these things. Some of it is from the trial transcript but most is from oral history. It makes a lovely story that she was ecstatic in the fire but believers, or even good storytellers, would have made her that way.

The part I understand is where she stopped listening and took things into her own hands. Because I am doing that now. I got ahead of God. I am sitting here in the redwood prison waiting for him to catch up.

I hear a sound that is not a forest sound. Or maybe it is. Sounds mix together here. Birdsong mixed with the snapping of twigs mixed with external danger mixed with internal peace. But this is a strange shuffling, like an animal engaged in a hunt. I look up and see Willie looming in the fog and the fractured light.

CHAPTER TWENTY-SIX

Davvid doesn't want to admit why he is sitting in the waiting room of Dr. Heather Hensen. He is telling himself that it is a desperate attempt to find Sarah, based on what Emily has told him. A woman in a fragile state, a former patient, is wandering around in the world with a dangerous man in an even more unstable condition. He has to know that he tried. He has to make a move, even one as unlikely as this.

But there's something else to it. There is a feeling. He can't describe it. It's more like a compulsion and David Sutton does not get compelled. He has often felt so in charge of his impulses that he has had to reach to understand his patients with chemical dependencies and other kinds of compulsions. He has to meet them on a logical terrain, a landscape of scientific evidence. It is his own version of a leap of faith since he can't experience it. But now he is experiencing it. He had to come here. His attempts to argue with himself were futile. He applies no credence to what Heather Hensen does and he knows she won't be able to help him break down the puzzle of where Sarah has gone but it doesn't seem to matter.

He's terrified that he might confess some of this to Heather Hensen. He's terrified that this will turn into some kind of therapy session for him. He feels sick when he imagines himself opening up to her and making himself vulnerable to someone he considers a charlatan at best, a self-deceived mental case at worst. His stomach is roiling and he is thinking of leaving when the door opens and there she is.

"Dr. Sutton. I had a feeling I was going to hear from you again."

"What do you mean?"

"I mean you've been on my mind."

"Why?"

She smiles that guileless smile that employs her whole being. Her gray-blonde hair is swept back into a ponytail and her eyes are green, like sea glass, and for the first time it hits him that she looks very much like Sarah Lange. They have the same features but their demeanors differ greatly. Sarah seems more grounded, more serious, with a penetrating gaze and an unnerving calm. Heather seems like she might float away and take you with her. David doesn't know where these kinds of thoughts are coming from. They are new to him.

"Maybe we can go into my office before we begin the debate?" Heather asks.

He stands and tucks his head and walks past her without looking at her.

Once he's in the calm room with the soft light and the trickling water, he feels even less himself. Something is blooming inside of him, a strange sense of calm mixed with excitement mixed with dread, all fighting to take charge. He feels as if something is awakening in him that he hasn't known since childhood. He cannot name it. He does not want to name it.

"Let's start from the beginning," she says, sitting across from him. She is wearing perky athletic clothes, like last time. Why does this irritate him? Or is that irritation? He can't name the feeling, like all the other feelings warring it out inside him.

Mad, sad, glad, afraid. These are the options they sometimes boil it down to for their patients. To help them narrow the field. But why those, he wonders. And why only one positive option? There are so many more emotions and he suddenly finds he can't identify his own and he also suddenly realizes that emotions are forces, like energies, that invade and take over. Not just a wiring in the brain, a conversation between neurotransmitters. It feels like something greater than that. It feels. That is the point.

"The beginning?" he asks her, finally raising his eyes to hers.

"Yes. How are you?"

"Oh. I'm…"

He can't finish the sentence. She lets him off the hook. "How is Sarah?"

"She has disappeared. She ran away from the facility with another patient."

"Yes, I heard. But I assumed you'd found her."

"Why would I find her?"

"Well, I mean the police. Someone."

"No. No one has found her. But it's a difficult situation and I was hoping you could help."

She cocks her head. Her smile disappears but her face is still open and welcoming. Her resting expression is one of grace. This is the best word he can find.

"How can I help?" she asks.

"I'm not sure yet. I thought we might start with her favorite places. Retreats. Anywhere she liked to go back when you knew her. Did that ever come up?"

"Sure. She did like to go away to write and work. She had a handful of favorite spots."

"Do you remember?"

"New York was her favorite."

David shakes his head. "I don't think she went to New York. It has to be driving distance."

"Why?"

"Because we've checked with the airlines."

"Have the cops followed her credit card transactions?"

"No. The cops aren't really interested anymore. It takes resources to follow up and this one isn't high priority."

Heather barely moves. She watches him for a long moment, then recrosses her legs in a manner that is meant to signify nothing.

"Well, she likes the desert. She sometimes went to Palm Springs, Ojai. Sometimes drove up the coast to Big Sur or Carmel."

"How far north did she go?"

Heather shrugs. "She never mentioned anything beyond Carmel."

"Carmel," he says. "Was that a favorite spot?"

"She didn't really have a favorite spot."

David sighs and looks at his hands. Heather leans forward in her chair. "Why are you taking this on yourself?" she asks.

David feels exposed and blames himself for feeling that way. He avoids her eyes.

"Look, I know," he says, trying to locate his professional voice. "I know her whereabouts are not really my responsibility."

"And yet," Heather says.

"And yet it feels like my responsibility."

"Because?"

"Stop," he says. "I didn't come here for a session."

Heather leans back in her chair.

"What did you come here for then?" she asks.

"I don't know. To try. To do something. To help. I don't know."

She waits. David thrashes around in his own brain.

"I was looking for…I don't know…I had questions. The two of you seemed to have a common language"

"Really."

"Yes."

Heather shifts in her chair and addresses her ponytail and takes a sip of water and stares at him.

"Do you have a romantic interest in her?"

"No, this isn't about sex."

"I didn't say sex. I said romance."

He actually rolls his eyes but it doesn't faze her.

"Are you making an ideal out of her, Dr. Sutton? Damsel in distress, dragon in the cave, that kind of thing?"

"No. I don't do that."

She smiles and crosses her arms and he has a bizarre impulse to shake her. He doesn't understand this effect she is having on him. She is pushing buttons that have never been pushed. He has to look away from her and he knows she is noticing that, too.

"Look," she says, "Sarah is a magnet."

"I'm sorry, what?"

"She is magnetic. It's inside her. She is inner lit. People gravitate to her. Especially broken people."

"I'm not broken. I'm her doctor."

"I didn't say you."

"And she's not magical."

"I didn't say that. But she has had a metaphysical experience. She has glimpsed something. She knows something."

"She is certifiably insane."

"When I worked with her she was not."

"Was she talking to guides then?"

Heather stares at him as she processes her thoughts and chooses her words carefully.

"That is more common than you'd imagine," she says.

"Really."

"Because a lot of people tap into a strong inner guidance. They have prophetic dreams or they see a dead loved one or hear a detached voice. Most people, I'd say, have had some kind of experience like that."

"I disagree."

"We are like radios, Dr. Sutton, and sometimes the lower and higher frequencies break through. Some people are more sensitive than others to those frequencies. Machines are made in our image. How could they be otherwise? How could you think that particles and waves and electrical impulses bounce all around you and operate or affect your machinery but not you?"

"I don't know."

Heather leans forward. "What if Sarah's not crazy?"

"She's suicidal."

"What if she's suicidal because people keep telling her she's crazy?"

"She's homesick for Heaven."

"Maybe that's just her language for 'exhausted.' Maybe she's a poet."

David looks at her. "I had a thought like that."

"Oh?"

"Yes. I had a thought that maybe she abandoned her purpose."

"Purpose? You believe in something like that?"

He thinks of Joe and his talk of charisms. He feels confused and out of sorts. Heather is not helping matters, the way her stare is bearing down on him.

He shakes his head. He feels her watching him. "You know what they tell us, in the earliest stages of our profession."

"They tell us a lot of things," she says.

"People would rather die than change," he says.

She nods, pressing her fingers to her lips. Something about this motion encourages him.

"But maybe it's not that people would rather die than change. Maybe people would rather die than…" His voice trails off.

"What?" she asks.

"Than step into themselves."

His voice doesn't even sound like his. But the way her eyes light up makes him want to own that voice and that thought.

"People would rather die," she says, "than be free?"

He shakes his head vigorously. "No," he says. "Than belong."

She thinks about it. He can't bear the weight of her thinking about it.

He sighs and begins gathering his things.

"Doesn't your struggle ever wear you out, Dr. Sutton?"

"Of course. Doesn't yours?"

"Yes, but I know how to step out of it."

"That must be fun for you."

"And I'm not in charge of it."

"So you're at the mercy of it?"

"More like I'm in the middle of it."

Now he is standing. "I'm sorry I came here."

She follows him to the door and they reach for the door handle at the same time and their hands touch and something shoots through him that he can't name. Revulsion, he wants to believe, but it isn't.

She takes her hand away and says, "If she's driving she probably went up the coast. Not down. And I agree it's unlikely she got on a plane."

"Yes. Thank you."

"Good luck."

"I don't believe in luck."

"Neither do I. It's an expression."

"Goodbye," he says.

"I don't believe in goodbye," she taunts after him and he resists turning around.

CHAPTER TWENTY-SEVEN

As kidnappers go, Willie is a hospitable one. He keeps going to the minibar and bringing me food, little feasts of miniature Reeses and smoked almonds. He tries to give me alcohol but I don't take it. I just watch him chug one little bottle after another, like magic love potions. I am waiting for them to do their trick so I can figure out how to get out of this situation.

He hasn't tied me or anything. He doesn't need to. A couple of times when I ran for the door he pushed me so hard it winded me. The second time I hit my head and was unconscious for a little while. I'm entirely convinced that Willie can kill me now, so I decide not to test him anymore.

He is in a big leather armchair watching a movie on TV and I am in the armchair beside him and there is a fire in the fireplace. It is a homey scene, all but for the hostage factor, and the coziness of it disorients me and makes it difficult for me to think. On the one hand my heart is racing like a meth addict and on the other I feel comfortable and reassured by the pop of the fire and the drone of the TV and even the taste of chocolate and nuts in my mouth.

I could use the guides about now. But they have gone completely silent. Every attempt to contact them leaves me feeling more defeated. My prayers are like bodies thrown down a well. I don't even hear them land. I know this is my fault. It is because I went off the path and it is because I felt I had better ideas and now I'm left to my own ideas. It's not a punishment. It's permission. Do it your way, they are saying to me. Have at it. And now that I don't want to do it my way I can't hear them because I am so afraid. There is a reason that the angels and Jesus and the burning bush and every other heavenly representative said, "Be not afraid." In fact, I read somewhere that it is the most often repeated phrase in the scriptures. But being not afraid is like trying not to think of a white bear or whatever the adage is. Fear builds on itself. It is a vortex and once you are in it you just spin and flail around. I am in it.

A memory swims to the surface of a time when I was young, in college or just after, when I was denying my history and my experience and joining the merry band of intellectuals, when we were all atheists and socialists and scientists and we were going to take it from here. When I was running my own life in the most literal and dualistic way and I somehow made it work. It's not as if I was unhappy then. Quite the opposite. There is a kind of security in knowing that you're at the helm and as long as you keep your wits about you things will be fine, perhaps even perfect. The reason you can go with that theory for so long in your twenties and, if you are lucky, well into your thirties, is that nothing much happens to you. Then things begin to happen to you. Things you did not organize, things you could not have predicted, things that bring you to your metaphorical and sometimes literal knees. Like a guy crawling in your apartment window and raping and nearly killing you. My intellect did not line that up and couldn't do much to get me out of it.

In this instance, sitting in front of the fire with a bipolar potential murderer, I have to give my intellect almost full credit. This was my idea. So it stands to reason, I think, that my intellect should be able to get me out of it. I am forced to go with logic, survival instincts, situational awareness, and strategy. The problem is that I haven't relied on those things in so long. I barely know how to conjure them. It's like trying to start a car that has been rusting on the front lawn for years.

This is no time for dissecting my psyche but I do it anyway.

Why am I here with Willie? Because I felt a desire to save an artist. This is why I believe I came back. Well, to be fair, I never thought about why I came back until Dr. David Sutton brought it up. I try to dial it back to an instinct that might be more pure, less influenced by the doctor. What was happening the first time I saw Willie?

He was looking for red wool for his art piece.

Why was he looking for red wool?

He wanted to depict a woman being killed by a shark.

So I was drawn to an artist who was deprived of expression.

Or I was encountering a man who wanted to kill a woman.

Questions, I think. Begin with questions. That's what Socrates did.

What is his plan? What does he want out of this situation?

"Willie," I say as evenly as I can. "Do you know how long you want to stay here?"

He turns his head slowly away from the TV. "What?"

"I was just wondering if you had an idea of how long you want to be here."

"No."

"Do you want to call Emily?"

"No."

"Are you hungry for real food at all? Because we could get room service."

"No, no," he says and his voice rises a little and I can see irritation building.

I back off and we stare at the TV screen for a little while.

"Do you know what movie this is?"

"No."

The questions might have worked for Socrates but they are getting me nowhere.

"Willie," I say, "I would really like to go home."

He slams his hand on the coffee table and glares at me.

"Stop talking to me," he says. "I can't think. My head is full of noise."

"What kind of noise?"

"Just noise. Like static. I told you. I want to put you through a wall. I am trying to decide if I am going to do that or jump off a bridge."

"Why does that have to happen?"

"One of those things has to happen and if you don't shut your fucking mouth you'll decide for me."

I shut my fucking mouth and stare into the fire.

I am just like everyone else. I am at the mercy of others. I am stranded with my thoughts and my thoughts are scattered and unhelpful. I am praying to a God I can't hear, that I don't believe in anymore, and my desperate mewling makes me feel weak and disgusting. If I were an omnipotent God I wouldn't listen to me either. I'd be thinking, *Oh, really, now you need me? You're so smart, figure it out.*

I sink back in my chair and get quiet and try to find another scrap of logic.

I can remember my friends, Laurie and Samantha. I can remember my ex-fiancé, Ben. I can remember that the first time I saw Willie, he was trying to create a piece of art depicting a dead woman.

If you can't remember what you came back for, said Dr. David Sutton, you might be unaware of your purpose.

You are an artist, he said.

Was, I said.

Are, he said.

A true seer, a prophet of her century.

From where I sit I can see into the bathroom and I see a telephone on the wall. I try to keep my breathing slow and quiet.

"Willie, I need to go to the bathroom."

"Yeah, okay."

I get up and make my way there.

"Leave the door open," he says.

"I'd rather…"

"Leave the fucking door open, cunt."

I pretend to use the toilet and then I flush it and while it is flushing I pick up the telephone receiver.

"How may I help you Mrs. Rabbit?"

"Please send help," I whisper. "Help me."

Willie turns his head toward me and stands. I scramble to put the phone back.

I pull up my jeans and flush the toilet again and walk toward him so he won't come into the room.

"Who were you talking to?" he asks.

"No one."

"You were talking to someone."

"Myself. I'm crazy, remember? Jesus, Willie, I just wanted to pee by myself.

It's over. I'll come back to the fire now."

I walk back and he turns and follows me.

"I forget you're crazy, too," he says.

We sit in front of the fire for a long time and then someone is suddenly knocking on the door.

Someone says, "Mrs. Rabbit, did you call us?"

Willie looks at me. I try to shrug but even in the interest of survival my lying is bad. Willie walks to the door and stands right next to it and speaks.

He says, "We don't need anything, thank you."

"Someone called from the room," the voice on the other side says.

"No one called," Willie tells the voice.

"All right then," the voice says. "Do call if you need anything."

My shoulders are up around my ears. I try to get my body to relax. Willie turns and looks at me.

"You fucking cunt," he says. "You called somebody."

"No. I didn't."

He advances on me. He is six foot four and descending on me. I think about standing but find I can't, find it wouldn't matter if I could.

"Willie, please."

He is on me now. He puts his hands around my throat and lifts me up. I can't breathe. He is going to throw me through a window or something. He is going to catapult me. This isn't going to be some kind of typical dying scene. It is going to be spectacular, something beyond our imagining.

I suddenly recall living. I remember how to live and how to be and I want more of it. I am sorry for all the days I spent listening to the guides. I just want to be a normal person being alive. But I cannot draw a breath.

CHAPTER TWENTY-EIGHT

Out of nowhere, without warning, David and Jen have sex. They don't discuss it before or after. The fact that they are pretending it is normal for them to have sex makes him sad. In a reversal of roles, she falls asleep immediately after and he lies awake, staring at the ceiling, wanting to talk. He feels needy. His thoughts are racing. He is cycling wildly between thoughts of marrying Jen and breaking up with her. *This relationship is fine. You won't do better. It is dead. It has been dead a long time. It is dragging us both down. She knows me. I could get old with her. My family likes her. We are in the same field. I can talk to her. I can't talk to her. She only knows what I show her. I don't want to reveal myself to her. I don't trust her. She is dedicated to her profession. Her profession is a load of nonsense. She helps people. Do I help people? She has a good body for her age. For any age. She can take care of me. But she won't take care of me. All she does is work. But that is all I do, too. We are perfect...*

He begins to feel sleepy. He loves the feeling of sleep suddenly taking him under. It is like stepping out of the world. Heather Hensen said something to him like that. Doesn't the world ever wear you out? He feels worn out.

His eyes give way and then his body gives way and then he is in something like sleep. He goes into a dream and he is aware that he is dreaming. This rarely happens to him. In fact, he rarely remembers his dreams, which has always made self-analysis more difficult. But this is a dream, the kind that people talk about in his office, but more pronounced. He is on a winding road, a cliff, with a sharp drop to the ocean. He is on this road and he is not the driver but is inside the driver's head. He feels confused and at the same time excited. He is not afraid of going over the cliff. Something in him wants to go over the cliff. Then he goes deeper into the dream and almost loses the sense of dreaming and finds himself in a state of near reality, a swapping out of realities, and he is standing on a small beach and he is staring at a rock formation with a hole cut perfectly in the center of the formation. When the waves crash they explode through this hole and it is beautiful and dramatic and specific. He knows this is a real place. He does not want to move from the beach but suddenly he wants to run from the beach and when he tries, his feet start to sink in the sand. His breath is coming in labored fits and he wants to scream and can't do that either.

He starts awake and sits up in bed. Jen doesn't move.

He gets out of bed and goes into his study. He begins rifling through the books in his library. He has some picture books about California and he finds the one he is thinking of and begins flipping through the photographs. He is looking for the rock formation. He is certain it is a real place and he has seen it before.

Finally he comes upon it. Pfeiffer Beach in Big Sur.

He turns on his computer and brings up all the hotels in Big Sur and begins calling them. On the second try he reaches The Ventana Inn. No, the woman says, they don't have a guest by the name of Sarah Lange or Willie Cranston. He describes them to her. He is very tall and she is short and pretty and blonde and—he wants to say ethereal but stops himself.

"You might have noticed something a little exceptional about them," he says instead. "An odd couple."

"Well, that sounds like Mr. and Mrs. Rabbit. The staff has been amused by them since they got here. In fact, we just got a strange call from their room."

"What was strange about it?"

"Wait, who are you, sir?"

He explains his situation.

"Well," she says, "there was a call from their room. The woman was asking for help. So we sent someone but when they got there, the guests wouldn't open the door. Mr. Rabbit said they were fine. We tried calling, too, but no one answered."

"And you just left it at that?"

"We can't just go into a guest's room, sir."

"Even if a woman is in distress?"

"The woman didn't say she was in distress. And Mr. Rabbit said everything was fine."

"She said she needed help."

"Guests often say they need help. With the fireplace or the cable."

"Did it sound like she was worried about cable?"

"We've had no reports of noise or struggle in their room."

"Is the hotel full?"

"No, sir."

"So they probably don't have any neighbors to report such sounds."

"Sir, people come here for a lot of reasons. We are a kind of sanctuary."

"You are a hotel. Churches and embassies are places of sanctuary."

"What would you like us to do?"

"Send someone back there."

"Sir..."

"And call the police. You don't understand. This man is dangerous. Her life is in danger."

There is a protracted silence followed by some mumbling.

"All right," she finally says.

"Call me back immediately."

"Yes, sir."

He hangs up and a feeling of panic comes over him. That she may be dead. That he might be crazy. That he's doing all this based on a dream. He doesn't even believe in dreams in this way. He doesn't want to know what it all means. He hopes he is wrong. He wants to go back to not knowing.

He knows there is no going back.

CHAPTER TWENTY-NINE

So for the second time in my life a man is choking me and I leave my body and hover somewhere around the ceiling and watch it unfold.

Why does this keep happening? Why am I trying to die this way?

You are homesick for Heaven.

Where have you been?

You wanted to do this your way.

I don't want it anymore. I want to come back and I want to stay there and I want to know what it feels like to be normal. I want to live on Earth and play nicely with others and see what they see and hear what they hear and do what they do.

Are you sure?

Yes. No. Let me think about it.

You don't have much time.

I will think fast.

Then there is a banging and then everything hurts.

CHAPTER THIRTY

His hand trembles as he dials Emily's number.

Her voice is foggy.

"This is Dr. Sutton," he says.

"Yes?"

"They found them."

"Who found them?"

"I found them. It's a long story. They're in Big Sur."

"Are they okay?"

"She's alive but injured. They've taken her to the hospital. He's okay but they took him into police custody."

There is a deep silence and he hears her sigh.

"What happened?" she asks.

"I don't know."

"You didn't ask?"

"They don't know. I'm going to Big Sur."

"Big Sur?"

"That's where they are. Do you want to come with me?"

"Yes," she says. "Of course."

She gives him her address and he hangs up without saying goodbye. He fumbles in the dark for some paper and a pen to leave Jen a note. He doesn't want to wake her. She has trouble sleeping lately and he doesn't want to disturb her. This is what he tells himself. He wants to kiss her but he is afraid. He wants to marry her. He wants to leave her. His mind will not settle. He is glad to have something else to think about.

He leaves her a note saying where he is going and that he will call when he gets there.

Emily meets him in front of her apartment building. She is pacing. She is wearing a leather jacket and a scarf and is carrying a messenger bag.

"I didn't know how to dress," she says, getting into the car. "Is it cold there? I don't even know where it is besides north. And there are winding roads. And people go there to drop out. Henry Miller, right? Kerouac. People like that."

"Yes."

"How far is it?"

"Five hours or so."

"Are you going to be like this the whole time?"

"Like what?"

"Monosyllables."

"What would you like to talk about?"

"I don't know. Nothing. I should probably sleep. Or listen to music. Can you turn on the radio?"

He does and she puts her head against the glass and after a few minutes she's quiet and he stares at the dark road. He wonders why he didn't, or doesn't, call the hospital in Carmel himself and ask about Sarah's condition and find out what happened. There is only one answer. He isn't prepared to know yet.

"Are you married?" Emily asks.

The voice startles him. "No."

"Why?"

"I don't know."

"Are you gay?"

"No."

"You've just never wanted to get married."

"I've always wanted to in the abstract. Never in the specific."

"What does that mean?"

"I like the idea of it."

"But not the reality."

"I always imagined that getting married requires a kind of compulsion. That it's not a decision but a kind of dawning. Suddenly it's clear and you move. But I think that's a naïve concept."

"It's not naïve. It's romantic. Are you a romantic, Dr. Sutton?"

"Not at all. I would have thought."

He remembers Heather Hensen asking him the same thing and it makes him uncomfortable. He remembers how she unsettled him and he pushes the memory away.

"Except about marriage," Emily says.

"I just wanted something to take it out of my hands."

"Like God?"

"Like chemistry."

"You want a chemical marriage?"

"I want to feel compelled. I want to be moved."

"And you're not a romantic."

"I don't think passion is a romantic concept. I think it has something to do with the neurotransmitters. With the evolution of the species. In fact, what we call passion is probably more like physics."

"Physics?"

"Electromagnetism."

"Wow. Hard to believe no one has snapped you up."

He laughs.

"It laughs," she says.

"What's your perspective on it?" he asks. "Were you caught up? Or it was a logical decision?"

"It was both. He was going away to art school and we were caught up."

"How old were you?"

"I was twenty, he was twenty."

"You couldn't have just moved to art school with him?"

"It was in North Carolina. I had this idea that people wouldn't appreciate a cohabitating couple down there. And I was sure, so why not?"

"Was he sure?"

"He was after I got through with him."

He laughs again.

There is a moment of silence where he lets his next question form. And she seems to be waiting for it.

"Were you ever worried…?" he asks.

"Yes."

"That you…"

"Wanted it more than he did?"

"I wouldn't have phrased it that way."

"Give me your version."

"That you persuaded him."

"What's the difference?"

"I was talking about timing, not an imbalance in the relationship."

"We'll never know," she says quietly.

He doesn't jump to fill the silence, though he wants to. He wants to reassure her though he has no idea why.

"The thing is," she says, "we had a deal. He would be the artist and I would work to support him. He wouldn't have to teach or wait tables or anything. He could just concentrate on his work. And I believed he would make it. I always believed that. It was just a matter of time."

"What was his medium?" David asks, hating the stiffness of the question and its past tense but not knowing how else to phrase it.

"Everything. But mixed media in particular. He did this series of shadow boxes that were full of antiquated science equations and equipment. They were on display at MOCA for a while. He got a grant after that. Then a couple of celebrities found him and he was getting commissions."

"When was that?"

"A couple of years ago."

"What happened?"

"Crazy. Crazy happened."

"Do you think it was related to his success?"

"No, I think it was a mind-boggling coincidence."

He says nothing.

"I'm sorry," she says.

"It's all right."

"Here's the thing. Do you want to know the thing?"

"If you want to tell me," he says.

"Do you ever turn off the shrink thing?"

"I don't know."

"Okay, here's the thing. Because I made all the money for so long, I managed the bank accounts and I took care of the rent and the cars and insurance and appliances and you name it. I took care of the details. And one day Willie wasn't a young guy anymore. He was a guy approaching forty who didn't know how to make a plane reservation. And it scared him. But it didn't scare me. Because now it didn't matter who wanted it more. He couldn't leave. I did that to him."

David says nothing.

"I shackled him," she says.

She begins to cry quietly. He wants to reassure her again but still he doesn't and he lets the sound of her weeping fill up the car like a different kind of music.

CHAPTER THIRTY-ONE

I have a TV in my room. I haven't watched one in a focused way in a very long time. I flip the channels and I can't help marveling. What is this? Is this what people like? There's a lot of shouting. There are hundreds of shows about dead people and how they got that way. The rest are about rich people and pretty people and how they got that way. It's hard to look away from it. I see why people get addicted. But I also feel it infecting me. It starts to feel like a window and you start to believe these people are the norm and are everywhere and this little box of a world is all there is. It helps you forget. I want to forget right now. I'm too ashamed to do anything else.

A nurse comes in and says, "Someone is here to see you."

"Who would come to see me? I don't have anyone."

"Your doctor."

"I just saw the doctor this morning."

"Your other doctor," she says and there is a hint of something like embarrassment in her voice.

Dr. David Sutton walks in. He is wearing jeans and a tweed jacket and a button-down shirt. This must be his traveling look. It makes me smile. My smile, I can see, unsettles him.

He pulls up a chair and sits next to me.

"How are you?" he asks.

"Well, I'm pretty damn crazy, wouldn't you say?"

He doesn't laugh.

"How do you feel?"

"My throat hurts. My head hurts. I'm tired. I feel like someone tried to kill me. Why are you here?"

"I came with Emily. I brought her here."

"Willie's wife."

"Yes."

"And where are they?"

"He's in jail. She's bailing him out."

"What's he charged with?"

"I don't know. Nothing will be official until the arraignment."

"I don't want him charged with anything."

"That won't be up to you."

"Really? Even though I'm the one who nearly died?"

Dr. Sutton sighs and shifts in his chair and is very annoyed with me. I don't need any help to understand that.

"Are they going to arrest me, too?" I ask.

"What for?"

"Stealing the truck."

"No. Oceanside is not going to pursue that."

"And I kidnapped a patient."

"Everything's under control. You're going back there and I'm going to continue treating you."

"Wow. People just cut a wide path for the crazy, don't they?"

"Please stop referring to yourself that way."

"I'm on your side. I'm ready to admit it."

"Do you want to talk to me about what happened?"

"Why I kidnapped Willie?"

"Yes, we can start with that."

"Can I have a drink first?"

"They don't have alcohol here."

"You really have lost your sense of humor."

He doesn't respond.

"Okay, Dr. Sutton. It went like this. I decided Willie was dying in there. I decided he was a great artist and he needed to answer that calling and the drugs and the shock treatments were interfering and if I could just get him away I could cure him. I thought I was divinely inspired."

"Did the guides tell you to do that?"

"No. That's the problem."

"Can you elaborate?"

"I stopped listening to them and went into business for myself. Or maybe they just stopped talking and I tried to fill the void. See, the way it is with Heaven, you either do their business or your business. But you don't interpret what they want. You don't get creative. You don't anticipate. You can't get ahead of Heaven. That's what I did."

"I see."

I take a deep breath. I'm ready to say this. I know when I say it, it will be permanent.

"And now I'm like you."

"What do you mean?" he asks.

"I'm normal. I don't hear the voices anymore."

"Since when?"

"Since I left. Oceanside. No, a little before."

"And why do you think that is?"

"I don't know. Maybe I snapped out of it. Maybe it can happen like that. Crazy can just one day be over like a virus."

He smiles but I can see he doesn't believe me. Of course he doesn't. I've been yammering to him about spirit guides for...how long now? I still can't do math. But that's who I am to him.

He says, "Sarah, maybe we can take this moment to make a connection."

He has called me Sarah. Even he doesn't seem to hear this. But I do.

"Sure. I've always felt connected to you," I say.

"Not between you and me. Between what happened back then and what happened a few days ago."

I have a moment of no earthly idea what he's talking about. Then I recall the moment of clarity I had when Willie was trying to choke me. Twice in one life. Probably not a coincidence. This is what Dr. Sutton is struggling to say.

"Oh," I say. "I hear you."

"We don't have to go deeply into it now."

"But you're wondering why I keep trying to get myself killed in the same way?"

He scratches his chin and doesn't answer. He looks away from me and toward the window where the afternoon light is fighting its way through the blinds.

I can tell something is different about him, though. His body language, the way he has trouble looking at me, the way he fidgets with his keys.

"What is it?" I ask.

"What is what?"

"You're acting strangely."

"I've been through an ordeal."

"My ordeal?"

"Yes. I'm in it with you."

"No, you're not."

"I'm your doctor."

"You guys don't get emotionally involved, do you?"

"We compartmentalize. It's not the same as not caring."

"Dr. Sutton, are you a little in love with me?"

The question throws him off. He can't look at me.

"It's okay if you are," I say.

"No, I don't think that's it. I think it's bigger than that."

"Tell me."

"I can't. I'm not sure I understand it."

His cell phone goes off. His ring is some kind of classical music. He ignores it.

"What is that?" I ask.

"My phone." He reaches into his pocket for it.

"No, the music."

"It's Mozart. Eine kleine Nachtmusik. I'm sorry, I'll just turn it off."

"Don't you need to answer it? It's all right."

He looks at the screen. "I should answer it."

"It's all right."

He walks across the room and lowers his voice as if I won't be able to hear him. "Hello? Yes, I'm here. I'm all right. I was going to call. I had to see her first. She's fine. I mean, she's not fine but she's going to be all right, physically."

There's a significant pause.

"Listen to me," he says. "Calm down. She's a patient. You're not being rational. No, I don't have a savior complex, Jen. I'm a doctor. No, you're not. Look, you haven't really been yourself since the ordeal and I don't think the medication is helping. What do you mean? I'm trained to make judgments like that. Don't push me on this matter. Because I will say things I'll regret."

Another pause.

"No, not that. I'll ask you to stop pretending that we are in the same profession. I had ten years of medical training before I hung a shingle and you read a book and took a test online. A long time, Jen. I've felt that way a very long time. I've always felt that way. But it's not important. Because I don't need to approve of your profession. I don't need to like it. You need to like it but it seems you don't anymore if you ever did. Can we please talk about this later? It sounds like you've been drinking. No, I'm not keeping score. My point is that we should discuss this at a more appropriate and less emotionally charged time. Yes, I am always a shrink because you know why? I'm a shrink. I have to go. Call a friend. Have someone come over. You shouldn't be alone."

He ends the call and puts the phone back in his pocket. He keeps his back turned to me for a long moment. When he turns, I am flipping through a magazine and pretending to be engaged. I have no idea who anyone in the magazine is but the headlines seem to assume I do. It assumes that I care if the marriages of celebrities are on the rocks. It assumes I need to know where to buy the most flattering jeans and how to lose my belly fat in ten days. I put my hand on my belly to see if there is any fat. I can't tell. It seems to move more than it used to.

"I'm sorry," he says.

"What for?"

"Taking the call. She was worried. I told her I'd call when I got here."

"Jennifer."

"Yes."

"Do you live together?"

"No. But we were together when I left my house. She's there now. She's in a fragile state. I'm sorry, it's very unprofessional to reveal all this."

"It's okay. She's jealous."

"No. Not in the traditional sense. Just of the idea that I rushed to your side and left her alone. There's some professional jealousy going on. I guess that's how I'd describe it."

"I see."

"I don't mean to share this with you."

"Why not?"

"I'm here for you. My life is suspended when I'm in session."

"We're not in session."

"No. But I am here in a professional capacity."

"If you say so."

He sits back down in the chair and holds his spine straight and tries to breathe some professionalism back into it. He takes his glasses off and rubs his eyes and puts them back on, then interlaces his fingers in his lap and looks at me and waits.

"What?" I ask.

"Is there anything else you want to discuss right now?"

"Not really."

"Any questions?"

"When are they kicking me back to the crazy palace?"

"Tomorrow. I will escort you back myself."

"All of us? In the same car?"

"No. Emily will make other arrangements. We're still not sure what they are going to do with Willie."

"Will he come back to Oceanside?"

"No."

"I hope they treat him all right."

Dr. Sutton stares at me. I've taken him aback but he's struggling not to show it.

"You do comprehend what occurred, don't you?" he asks.

"Besides him trying to kill me?"

"No, just that."

"I didn't take it personally."

He clears his throat. "All right, we will discuss this later. You need to rest."

"You need to rest, too. You look tired."

He ignores this. He stands and remains by my bed for a moment as if he's not quite sure of the appropriate parting gesture. There's something in his body language that suggests he wants to kiss me. Maybe just on the head or the cheek. But I can tell that's what he wants to do and his intellect is battling against it.

"Well, then," he says.

"Yes, well."

"I'll see you tomorrow."

"Yes, you will."

He starts away.

"I remembered my friends," I say, knowing it will make him turn and he turns.

"What?"

"I have two friends. At least. Laurie and Samantha."

He lets this settle into his consciousness.

"Do you want me to call them?"

"No. I just wanted you to know that I have them. I remember them."

"Okay," he says.

"Also, I am an artist."

This seems to mean more to him.

"Oh?" he asks.

"Yeah. I think maybe it's important. Maybe it's what I came back for."

He nods, hands in his pockets, staring at the wall.

Finally he looks at me. "Well, you don't need to decide this tonight," he says.

"Yeah, I know. It's just an idea I had."

"We'll talk about it next session."

"Okay."

He smiles and starts to walk out.

"A little night music," I say to his back.

He turns in the doorway. "Excuse me?"

"Eine kleine Nachtmusik."

"Oh, yes."

"That's what calls to you? A little night music."

"I'm not sure I understand."

"Well, it's your ringtone. It calls you."

"It's just a ringtone."

"You hear it, underneath everything, like a bit of distant music. And then the music gets louder and you like it so you turn it up louder until it's all you can hear. That's what it feels like."

"Like you're a radio," he says.

"Yes. And the trick is to keep the volume low. But you can't turn it off. No one can live that way."

He nods. He hears me. And he leaves still wanting to kiss me but it's not me. It's something bigger. He knows that now. He knows it's the music.

CHAPTER THIRTY-TWO

"Well, it's about time," David's mother says.

Jen's hand is extended across the table and everyone leans in to get a view of the three-carat diamond. David feels himself blushing even though he's glad of this moment, glad of the way his siblings are sitting up and paying attention, glad of his father's satisfied smile, glad of his mother's near foaming at the mouth, thinking of the wedding she'll help to organize and how she'll centralize herself in the affair. Glad of the way Jen seems so calm now, as if this were always the problem, and the solution has lifted the fog of anxiety and anger and nervous energy. She's still now. She's at peace. She knows who she is. She is a woman in the world with a diamond on her hand and a party to plan. She is the center of attention.

And he is the one who has made all this happen. He feels manly, even heroic, for bringing so many dreams to the point of realization with a simple question and a piece of jewelry. Only Sherry and Greta seem to fall just short of delight. They are happy because there's now a common language, another girl brought into the fray to help conspire and gossip and complain about the men. But Sherry senses the threat that Jen might get to the grandchild threshold before she does—there seems to be some doubt that she can get there at all—and Greta seems ready to salivate over the ring and the commitment and the thing she now realizes she has always wanted but doesn't have and can't get from her married boyfriend. Every married woman to her must feel like the enemy. A glint in her eyes says, "And he'll cheat on you, too, just wait."

Or he's imagining this. He's creating all this in his head to avoid confronting a feeling that is welling up inside of him like a storm. He thrashes to understand it. It is centered in his stomach and a little bit behind the eyes and as he bows his head to think about it, he realizes it is shame. He's ashamed of himself for jumping through this hoop. Ashamed for being glad. He feels he has lost. They have won. But what was the competition, he wonders? What was ever at stake? And how is committing to the woman he loves some kind of loss?

"Well, don't look so jubilant, Dr. Doom," his father says. It takes him a moment to realize he's being addressed.

"I'm sorry, what?"

"You look like you need to be given last rites."

The table laughs. Even Jen laughs. She gives his shoulder a quick massage.

"I don't blame him," she says. "I haven't been easy to live with lately."

"But you don't live together," Greta provides.

"Well, I was speaking figuratively."

"Where will you live?" his mother asks.

"We haven't decided."

"Where's the hitching post?" Rich asks.

"What do you mean?" David asks.

"The wedding. Where's it going to be?"

"Oh, I don't know."

"Back East, maybe," Jen says. "My family are all in New York. It might be easier."

"But the weather," Verna says. "You can't depend on it. I mean, if it's an outdoor wedding."

"I haven't even thought that far," she says. "This just happened last night."

"Where did he do it?" Sherry asks in a nostalgic tone.

"At Vito's, this old-school Italian restaurant we love on Ocean Park. They all know us there. So he gets down on one knee and everyone is watching and when I take the ring they all applaud."

"What if you'd said no?" Greta asks.

"I guess that would have been embarrassing for David."

She laughs but Greta doesn't.

"Did you think about that, David, before you did it?" his sister asks. "That she might say no?"

"Of course."

"It was a risk worth taking, right, Son?" his father chimes in. "Anything worthwhile is always a risk worth taking."

"Yes, sir," David agrees.

The cook begins to serve the roast beef and the Yorkshire pudding and green peas.

"This looks lovely, Flora," his mother says. "I've been feeling English lately. I wanted a traditional Sunday dinner."

Rich says, "Later there will be football hooligans and cross-dressing."

Everyone laughs. Then there is the sound of utensils on plates and an awkward silence blooms.

"We've missed you," Greta whispers to Jen, right before their father launches a new topic.

"Whatever happened with that Big Sur business?"

Jen stiffens a little. David does not look at her. "I don't know what you mean," he says.

"The girl you were treating who ran away with the psycho murderer."

David clears his throat and puts down his utensils and takes a sip of water.

"First of all," he says, "she is a woman. And the psycho murderer did not actually murder anyone and is being treated somewhere in Arizona. The charges against him were dropped."

"Why?"

"Because my patient was not interested in pursuing it. And given that and his psychological state, it just wasn't a case worth the D.A.'s time."

"So they will load him up on pills," his father says, "and eventually release him and he might attempt to murder someone else?"

"Possibly, Dad. Or they might actually cure his disease and he'll go on to live a productive life. That does occasionally happen in my profession."

"So you tell me."

"He cures people all the time," Jen says. "He cured the girl. Sarah."

"She's a woman," David insists again. "Why does everyone call her a girl?"

"It's just an expression, sweetie," his mother says.

"But it's so revealing. Someone with a mental condition is jettisoned back to childhood by general society. She's had a whole life, she's worked, she's been engaged. She's not a girl."

It is not until he stops talking that he realizes how the passion in his voice has erupted and is still resonating around the room. Everyone is staring at him except Jen, who is cutting her meat with intense concentration.

"Beg your pardon," his father says. "We will self-correct forthwith."

"Don't patronize me," David says.

"I don't mean to patronize," his father says. "But it comes with the territory, being a pater and all."

The silence occurs again and he feels Jen lean forward. He wants to stop her because he feels a moment of victory descending and he doesn't want to let it pass.

"But he did cure her, the woman," Jen says. "In a matter of months she was well enough to be released. And she's living on her own and working and doing very well. He doesn't even see her except on a checking-in kind of level. Isn't that right?"

"Not even that," he says. "She's moved away."

"As I understand it, she just had a brief psychotic break but she's fine now."

"Loaded up on drugs, I imagine," his father says.

"She's on a mild antidepressant," David says. "And we shouldn't be discussing it."

Jen says, "David explained that psychotic breaks are not that unusual. It happens to people under an extreme amount of stress. They are imminently treatable. It's not a life sentence. It's more like an episode."

"Please, Jen," David says quietly.

"I'm not talking about her specifically now," she continues. "Just your work in general. Psychiatry. He sees things that I don't get to see. Because I'm not a real doctor. I'm just someone who read a book and took a test online."

There's no malice in her voice.

"Don't sell yourself short, dear," David's mother says.

"I'm not. It's the truth. I'm not going to continue in my profession. I never really liked it very much. I always had a little bit of disdain for my clients," Jen admits.

"What will you do?" Sherry asks.

"I'm going to be a wife," she says, leaning into David. "And hopefully a mother."

"That's music to my ears," Verna says.

Sherry sinks into herself and Greta reaches for her wine.

"Well, all's well that ends well," his father says. "To quote the Bard."

"It'll all be fine in the end and if it's not fine, it's not the end," Jen says. "That's what I used to tell my clients."

"And they let you get away with it?" Rich asks.

Everyone laughs and some kind of equilibrium is restored.

David has a strange sensation of floating and looking down from the ceiling at this room full of anthropomorphic coincidences with their food and their clothes and their jewelry and their witty remarks and nervous laughter. This is where he lives. This is what he cannot escape.

"We forgot to toast," his father says, raising his glass. "To David and Jen and conjugal bliss."

"To bliss," Jen says.

And the glasses ring out as they touch. David knows it is a vibration of sound waves but for a moment he imagines it is something otherworldly, a chime from Heaven, some kind of celestial endorsement. Or warning. He finds he cannot drink to bliss, having no earthly understanding of it. No one notices when he puts his glass quietly down, untouched.

CHAPTER THIRTY-THREE

Montauk is at the end of the Long Island peninsula and so feels very much like the end of the earth. In fact, they call it The End. This is where I have landed. I am at The End.

In the winter it is enveloped in fog and wind and sometimes snow. It is extreme and dramatic by its nature and I enjoy it, letting the landscape demonstrate all the hysteria that once lived in my head. It's not my job anymore to create the magic. I let it unfold around me.

People say it is haunted. The inhabitants love to propagate that idea and I like it, too. There are Indian burial grounds and as we all know, wherever there are dead Indians there are ghosts and poltergeists and demons. I don't experience any of this, of course, because the volume has been turned down. I can barely imagine anymore and when I do, it is mostly memory, a conjuring of the past to make sense of it and see how it all happened and how it can now serve me. I am firmly rooted in this world. And I am not disappointed in it. The house is next to a wildlife reserve and we have six deer and a bunny who go in and out of the backyard as if they are our pets. They know us now and don't run when we come outside. They stare and go back to what they were doing.

I am speaking in plural because I have a boyfriend now. It's a relationship, like other people have. Most people have, I should say. We live together and we do what we do. He surfs in the morning and comes back home and paces on the balcony and talks business on his iPhone, hooked up to it by an earpiece. He is Greek and his skin is a beautiful latte color and he has strong muscles and intense features. His hair is long and dark and peppered with gray, even though he is five years younger than I am, and his eyes are also a latte color and close together, indicating his ability to focus. He is grounded and grounding. He doesn't let me wander too much. When he stares at me, if I start to drift, his eyes bring me back to where we live. He knows about my past but we don't discuss it much. And it doesn't seem to worry him except when I begin to ramble about some idea or another, a business I want to open, another hobby I want to take up.

"Write," he says when I do that.

And so I write. I write poems that rhyme and poems that don't. Elegiac phrases that mostly make sense when I read them out loud, next to the fire.

"Draw," he says, when the poems start to get rambling and nonsensical.

I draw in pen. I have a vast set of pens and I can use up an entire day choosing among them. Some have fat, stubby points that make delicious bleeding boundaries. Some have thin, austere points that make defined, imprisoning lines.

I cook a lot and I sew. These are the other activities, the ones that keep me corralled. They are not art, as far as he is concerned, and I don't let on that the colors and the textures and the way it all comes together feels like art to me. I don't let on that the smells and the tastes assault my senses and cause something like euphoria to well up in me. I just behave as if it is all a chore and I even complain sometimes about the work and the tedious nature of it. Tedium is good, he says. We all need a certain amount of it.

"Do you ever think about it?" he asked just last night. There was a thunderstorm and we built a fire even though it is mid-August and we sipped cocktails and stared at the flames and listened to the wood popping. It was inevitably romantic and in that atmosphere, the mind wants to know things it shouldn't know.

"Think about what?" I asked.

"How it was. When you were in the hospital."

"I try not to."

"Do you remember how it felt?"

"To be crazy?"

He nodded.

"Not really," I lied.

"Does it scare you when you look back?"

"Yes. So I try not to look back," I lied again. I look back often.

"Does it feel like you could go there again?"

"No. Why? Do you worry about it?"

"Not really," he said and I knew he was lying.

We have this beautiful, mutual lying routine.

"It's not a subtle thing, Ryan. It will be noticeable if it comes back. But it won't come back."

"All right."

"I won't let it. I know how it happened. I won't open the door to it again."

"Okay."

"Besides, I have that magic pill."

"You think it's really the pill keeping it all at bay?"

"I think it helps."

I don't really take a pill. I tell him I'm taking a pill to make him feel better.

He said, "Do you ever think about the doctor?"

"No."

"I mean, he did help you. He saved you in a way."

"He came and got me. I like to think I did the work myself."

"Yes, I suppose that's the case."

Maybe it is because he is Greek that Ryan (his mother is Irish) doesn't have much trouble with my past, with the idea of gods who speak and manipulate our world. Not in a literal sense, of course, but he can see things symbolically. He understands metaphor. This is how we met to begin with, in an art class in New York City. Metaphor and Meaning. Ryan was just dabbling in art but I had decided to turn to it. Turn back to it, I should say, since it is the thing I left behind long ago when I moved to Los Angeles and started trying to make a living. It was my calling and I left it out in the cold like a pet. It stood at the door and whimpered and I knew it was never going to stop until I let it in. So I let in.

Dr. Sutton always understood that. If only he had met me at the door with that information. If only he had said, "You are an artist. Just try being it instead of dying from it." But you can't skip steps. You have to take every bit of life from the beginning to the middle to, as we are promised, the end.

CHAPTER THIRTY-FOUR

When David runs into Heather Hensen it is not an accident. There is a coffee shop in the lobby of her building and he has been going there every day for lunch. When she finally walks in, he waits for her to catch his eye. He will take that as a sign. He has been thinking this way for a while now and it is disturbing.

When she sees him she does a double take and smiles and approaches.

"Dr. Sutton. What a surprise. Do you live in the area?"

"No."

"Oh. Well, they do make a nice tuna sandwich here."

"Will you join me?" he asks.

"Sure."

It is the kind of place where you order at the counter and pick it up and bring it to your table. So he has to wait while she does this.

He is sweating and his heart is pounding while he waits for her to return. He feels he is hanging onto a very thin reed on a very narrow ledge and it is slipping. He doesn't know what happens when he falls. He doesn't want to know. He doesn't even want to know why he is feeling this way and wishes he could stop it and has tried.

His visit to Father Joe a while back was not much help. This was the first place he went when he felt himself losing his grip. It was nothing outstanding, just a strange preoccupation with intuition and where a life of following it might lead. It might lead, he realized, to Jung, whose work he had always pretended to admire but actually dismissed and ridiculed in his heart. It had been comforting, the notion that everything was either in the will or in the definable branches of the brain. Mystery had had no place.

But he couldn't forget the dream. He couldn't explain the dream. He didn't want to think about the dream but he couldn't stop. Eventually, this sent him back to Joe.

"It's just the ineffable," Father Joe said to him. "I think you can live with that."

"What's the ineffable?"

"Everything. God and the rest of it. We can glimpse it but we can't fully reveal it. The problem with dismissing it is that you're living by a false construct. To say that we know it all? Well, it's just vanity."

"It's not that I think we know everything. It's that I think everything is knowable."

"Well, there's an astonishing distinction."

"I know it's subtle. Don't be an asshole."

"Reductionism. That's what you're talking about."

"Yes, my soul-searching can be reduced to that."

"Your soul?" Joe laughed. "Now you have a soul? You guys don't get to throw that word around. You're going with neurotransmitters, bags of chemicals. You don't get to play in the soul sandbox."

"Why are you antagonizing me?"

"I'm trying to get you to hear yourself. You came from nothing and you're going back to nothing but somehow everything you do in-between matters."

David had no answer for that. And he didn't know where else to go.

And he is still confused and can't believe that he has come here.

———————

Heather returns to the table with her food.

"I'm so excited," she says.

"About what?"

"The sandwich. The tuna sandwich. What did you think?"

"I don't know."

She sits and looks at him for a moment.

"Were you working up your nerve to come and see me?" she asks.

"Yes."

"You could have just made an appointment."

"I was afraid of doing that."

"Why?"

"I don't know. I don't know why I'm here. Something has happened to me."

"I heard about Sarah. She's all right now?"

"Yes, I think so. I don't hear from her. She was all right when she left."

"So something has happened since then."

"No."

"No?"

"Something happened before," he says under his breath.

Heather hears him. She says, "Tell me."

He launches into the Big Sur dream.

She nods and waits as if there is more. When he doesn't speak she leans back in her chair and crosses her arms.

"Wow. You've never had an experience like that."

"No," he says. "Of course not."

"Why 'of course not'?"

"Because I don't believe in it."

"If you didn't believe in gravity, would you expect to go floating into space? What is it with you people and belief? Why do you even talk about it?"

He feels cotton-headed and even a little like crying, so he quickly shifts the subject.

"Look," he says, "I want to come and see you. As a patient."

"Client."

"Client. Just a few sessions to hear you out and get into whatever this is."

"What do you think it is?"

"I think it's Generalized Anxiety Disorder because I'm getting married."

"Congratulations."

"Thank you. And ironically, my fiancé is, or was, a life coach, though she is much different from you. She's pragmatic. She sees it like training, the way you'd train a muscle. She created strategies for success and people followed them. Or not."

"We could do it that way. What would you like to be successful with?"

"Everything. Work. Marriage. I want to get back on track."

"Okay. What was the track?"

"I loved my job. Well, at least, I understood it. I want to understand it again."

"All right."

"And, of course, I want to be a good husband."

"Of course. Anything else?"

He thinks. It comes to his mind but he doesn't want to say it.

She says it for him: "You want to be happy."

"Doesn't everyone?"

"No, actually. But let's not worry about everyone else. Let's focus on you."

"All right."

She takes her phone out and starts scrolling on it.

"I have Tuesdays at two. Does that work?" she asks.

"Sure. I can make it work."

"And that happens to be right now so do you want to get started?"

"Oh." He looks at his watch and then his phone but he is stalling because he knows his day is free.

He feels something rush out of him and he thinks he might be dying. He stands in the threshold of this feeling and this moment and he knows he can only walk through the door and he knows he has to face it all, the known and the unknown and the new way of knowing and not knowing.

"All right," he says.

He releases his breath and bows his head.

"Well, you're not being led to your execution, Dr. Sutton. Just let me finish my sandwich."

She touches his hand. He raises his eyes to hers.

"It's going to be fine," she says.

And he believes her.

CHAPTER THIRTY-FIVE

This morning Ryan left for South Africa. He has some kind of business there. I don't really understand it. Something about nation-building but it is not God's work. He makes a profit. He travels all over the world and he worries about leaving me alone but I enjoy the space. He is a kind man, and faithful, and he takes care of me and he lets me take care of him, too. This is how it works with people, I now see. We take care of each other. We don't rescue. We take care.

Months have passed. I didn't feel them passing. It is the beginning of summer now. I think we came here in the summer so that means a year has probably passed. I should probably keep track of time. There's a reason people do that but I can't remember it anymore. I haven't needed to worry about time for a while. For quite some time.

But that's not entirely true. I keep track of time in the smallest of increments. Time for breakfast. Time for a walk. Time for dinner. Time for bed. Time for Ryan to come home. That kind of time. I'm starting to believe it's the only kind of time that matters.

The house feels vast and quiet when he leaves and I make sure to structure my day and find ways to fill it. Space is meant to be filled, not drifted upon. I walk into town to deliver my pies to the markets that sell them. Cherry and blueberry and peach. I also deliver the scarves and pillows and skirts that I sew by hand to the high-end boutique that keeps them in stock. It is fun to talk to the proprietors and we mostly discuss the weather and the surf and what Ryan is doing. They know us as the couple on the hill. We live in a large house on a gravel road, up the hill, behind the churches. There are two churches here, a large Catholic one and a smaller Lutheran one. The Catholic church is called St. Therese Lisieux. Little T. She was a nun who snuck into a convent at a very young age and took her vows and proceeded to be plagued by illness all her life. She prayed her way out of several conditions only to succumb to tuberculosis. She said, "I want to spend my time in heaven doing good on earth." So she is the patron saint of sick people. Any kind of sickness. You pray to her for health and well being and apparently she provides. Her presence is heralded by a single rose blooming. Wherever there shouldn't be a single rose. That is how she lets you know she is there and that your prayer has been answered. This is what they tell me. I have no experience of it, of course.

But I do think sometimes that this is why I found my way to The End in a town presided over by the patron saint of the sick. She keeps us well. It is her job.

After my chores are completed, I feel a compulsion to go into Southampton. I have been entertaining the idea of peddling my wares further in, to the tonier parts of the Hamptons. My handmade garments do well enough here but Montauk does not attract the fancier people. They tend not to travel much beyond Southampton. I could make a much better living there but it's not about the money so much. It is about stepping into my life as an artist, and that is also about not knowing. And not minding about not knowing. I believe they call it faith.

The train is not crowded going in this direction because it is a Thursday and most people are traveling to, not away, from the Hamptons. I like to sit and stare out the window at the landscape drifting past and I think about the fabrics I'd like to work with and the dinner I am going to make. It is okay to imagine these things because I will make them happen. They are more plans than visions.

The main street in Southampton is already crowded with weekend warriors. The women are talking in loud voices and the men are staring at their phones. The hyper energy of the city has not diffused yet. They are gearing up for fun and relaxation but they are not sure where it's going to come from and it creates an atmosphere of nervousness. I have to breathe through that. I can't afford to get caught up in their nerves. So I focus on visiting shops and I talk to a few owners and they show interest and I leave behind some samples and my card.

I think about getting something to eat here and remember there is a fancy delicatessen and maybe I can get some exotic spices and vinegars and oils while I am here. But before I can make my way there I am distracted by a beautiful outdoor flower mart. There are so many more varieties here than in Montauk. All kinds of roses and things brought in from the city so that the Manhattanites don't have to be too far from their creature comforts while they are desperately seeking decompression. I find the roses don't really speak to me, though, and it is still the local flowers that want to go home with me. I am drawn to the hydrangeas, even though I know I can get them back home, but there are a few more colors here. It is over a bright blue bouquet that I catch his eye. We stare at each other for a long time, as if we might have wandered into the same dream.

"Sarah?" he asks.

"Hello, Dr. Sutton."

He smiles and wanders over to me. He is wearing plaid shorts and a Polo shirt and the same Calvin Klein glasses and Top-Siders without socks. Something about his casual weekend look throws me. It's not the man I remember but somehow it is him.

"What are you doing here?" he asks.

"Shopping for flowers. What are you doing here?"

"Shopping for flowers," he says and we both laugh nervously.

"You look very well," he says.

"I am very well. You look like someone who doesn't really belong in the Hamptons."

He laughs. "I'm trying to be a good Roman."

"Well, maybe you'll grow into it. Do you live here now?"

"No, no. I'm here for the week. Just renting a place."

"Oh?"

"Yes, it's…the whole family is here. It's a gathering."

"Gatherings are nice."

"What about you? Do you live here?"

"Montauk," I say. "End of the line."

"Oh, I hear it's nice there."

"It is."

"Quiet."

"Yes. Quieter. Still the Hamptons."

"Right."

He is holding a large bundle of roses, pinks and reds.

"That's going to work," I tell him.

"What? Oh." He laughs. "Well, let's hope so."

"What did you do wrong?"

"Nothing. Yet. How about you?"

"I haven't done anything wrong today."

He laughs again. "No, I meant, are you with someone? Do you live alone?"

"I live with Ryan. I suppose he's my boyfriend. I never know how to describe it. We're in a relationship."

"That's good."

"Yes."

He stares at his feet for a moment and I want to rescue him from whatever is making him avoid my eyes. But I don't save anymore. I take care.

He looks up before I can even do that.

"Are you still an artist?" he asks.

"What?"

"The last time I saw you. You said you were an artist. You realized that about yourself."

"Yes. I guess I did."

"So you're doing that?"

"Yes."

"Are you making a living that way?"

I laugh into my fist. "No, not really."

He seems alarmed. "Why not?"

"It's not how I make a living. It's not about making a living." He nods and his face is a gathering storm of concern.

"I'm fine," I say. "I just don't need to burn down the cornfield with it."

"It seems a shame, though. I mean, if it's your calling."

"Look who's talking about callings."

"I mean your talent," he says. "Your gift."

"My charism?" I ask.

This word strikes something in him and his face comes completely to life. It is a look of profound recognition.

"Yes," he says. "Have you found your charism?"

I smile. "I believe it has found me."

"Even better," he says.

I hand him my business card and he stares at it for a long time.

"It's not as sad as all that," I say.

"No, I didn't mean…"

"Your expression. Like I've taken a wrong turn."

"Not at all."

"People need clothes. They need to eat."

"Of course."

"And I love providing those things."

"Yes."

"But what?"

"I didn't say but."

"Your face said it."

He shrugs and smiles.

"Dr. Sutton. You of all people should know there is more than one way of expressing art."

"Yes," he says. "I should know that."

I laugh. "You wanted me to be famous?"

His face processes a legion of emotions and finally he says, "I only ever wanted you to be happy."

"I thought you wanted me to be sane."

He shrugs. "Same thing."

"Really, doctor?"

"You have the strength to stand out," he says.

"And so do you."

"How do you know that?"

"Look at what you're wearing."

He looks down and blushes. "I thought I was fitting in."

"You're not exactly owning it."

He laughs and the blush deepens. He becomes preoccupied with the roses he is carrying, repositioning them, fiddling with the loud plastic wrapping paper.

"And you're still working at Oceanside?" I ask.

"Oh, no. I'm taking some time off. I might go back to school."

"For what?"

"Another discipline. I haven't decided. Maybe research."

"Sick of people and their problems?"

"I think the technical term is burnout."

"Did I do that to you?"

He shakes his head. "It was a long time coming."

"And when does this reinvention begin?"

"Maybe next spring. I'm taking some time off until after."

"After."

He seems hesitant to say the next thing.

"I'm getting married. That's why we're all here."

"Oh," I say, hearing the brightness in my voice and wondering if it sounds false. It's not meant to. It has little to do with him and his girlfriend, whom I don't know at all despite my speculations and the rumors at Oceanside. It has to do with marriage, the way someone who has failed to attempt it feels when the announcement is made. We all want them to fail, no matter how much we claim otherwise. We wish no one well because we cannot believe in the possibility of it, having destroyed the concept ourselves. That is how I used to feel anyway, and now I realize I am having a robotic response because something in me is experiencing the slightest lift, like a tiny champagne bubble struggling to find the surface. It is a new feeling, one of hope and good will. Not for the concept of sharing a lifetime, which still seems to me an unnecessarily punishing assignment, but for the optimism in the human spirit which comes up to bat again and again. I know this act must require a great amount of faith or surrender on Dr. David Sutton's part. And I know these aren't oceans he has ventured to swim in before. And I still think the unknown is a thing to step into if you can handle it. He won't just handle it. He needs it.

How do I know this? I know it. The way that any sentient being just knows a thing. Intuition. Feeling. Not magic. The voice that is always there, turned way down to an almost imperceptible volume, which is where it should stay.

"Congratulations," I say to him.

"Thank you. I'm glad I'm seeing you because I wanted to tell you. I didn't have your address. So this is a fine coincidence."

What must that feel like, I wonder. The idea that we are caught up in a series of coincidences.

Just as I'm thinking it, he says, "Or synchronicity."

I smile. "Listen to you."

"But it's awkward, what I wanted to tell you."

"Why?"

"Because of your part in it."

"I don't think I had a part in it. I never even met Jennifer. I saw her a couple of times but that's all."

"It's not Jennifer."

"It's not?"

"It's Heather."

I am rocked back for a moment. "Heather? Heather Hensen? My Heather?"

Suddenly it all settles like a light snow and it makes perfect sense.

"So, you see. You brought us together," he says.

He stares at me a moment longer and he seems to want to ask me something all important. Life altering, even. But to do so would be to negate our whole relationship, to turn the teacher into the student, the healed into the healer. I look away because neither of us is ready for that.

"I hope it's a wonderful wedding," I say.

"Thank you. Looks like the weather's going to be on our side."

"Yes."

He glances at his watch. "Well, I still have to go to the market. Everyone's probably thinking I engineered an escape."

"It's very nice to see you."

"And you."

We stare at each other and this time I am thinking of kissing him the way he was thinking of kissing me back in the hospital room. We are thinking of much more than that, too. We are thinking of a sharp turn that would send everything in the cart flying in all directions and we are both seeing some crazy tumultuous ride full of hills and valleys and storms and sunrises and tears and euphoria. It races back and forth between us like streaks of lightning and then it settles and fades and it never was.

"Goodbye, Dr. Sutton."

"Goodbye, Sarah."

I walk away without any flowers.

On the train ride home I stare at the landscape again and think of what I am going to make for dinner. Maybe I'll get some fresh corn from the market and turn it into a soup, a pale yellow sea of sweetness and warmth, chopped chives floating on top like little boats and just a touch cream, drifting across like a cloud.

CPSIA information can be obtained at www.ICGtesting.com
Printed in the USA
BVOW07s1345260913

332179BV00002B/18/P